"I could go by your house and check to make sure everything is secure, if it's okay with you."

Cassie had been so relieved to see the girls, she hadn't thought much about the continued threat to their safety. "Yes. Please. If you don't mind."

"I'll go by there now and meet you at the station." Turning to the girls, Brady called out, "I gotta go. Winnie is pretty jealous if I talk to other girls for too long."

Both Brook and Jilly laughed, but Cassie could hear the hollowness in their giggles. It made her chest ache and filled her with a righteous fury she wished she could rain down on Keith Norton. He'd not only stolen her girls, but he'd also taken away the precious safety and security they'd sought here in Jasper.

They had to find Keith Norton...

Or she would.

FOOTHILLS FIELD SEARCH

—

MAGGIE WELLS

For Sally, the Labrador we adore. Your search skills may be limited to an unerring ability to find food, but you certainly rescued us. Here's to all the pets and the people whose hearts they own.

Special thanks and acknowledgment are given to Maggie Wells for her contribution to the K-9s on Patrol miniseries.

Recycling programs for this product may not exist in your area.

ISBN-13: 978-1-335-48962-3

Foothills Field Search

Copyright © 2022 by Harlequin Enterprises ULC

For questions and comments about the quality of this book, please contact us at CustomerService@Harlequin.com.

Harlequin Enterprises ULC
22 Adelaide St. West, 41st Floor
Toronto, Ontario M5H 4E3, Canada
www.Harlequin.com

Printed in U.S.A.

By day **Maggie Wells** is buried in spreadsheets. At night she pens tales of intrigue and people tangling up the sheets. She has a weakness for hot heroes and happy endings. She is the product of a charming rogue and a shameless flirt, and you only have to scratch the surface of this mild-mannered married lady to find a naughty streak a mile wide.

Books by Maggie Wells

Harlequin Intrigue

Foothills Field Search

A Raising the Bar Brief

An Absence of Motive
For the Defense
Trial in the Backwoods

Visit the Author Profile page at Harlequin.com.

CAST OF CHARACTERS

Brady Nichols—Lieutenant with the Jasper Police Department. Search and rescue specialist. Left Boise in hopes of finding the home and future he wants in a small town.

Cassie Whitaker—A take-charge single mom who has moved to Jasper in search of a fresh start for herself and her daughters.

Winnie—Brady's K-9 partner, a two-year-old yellow Labrador retriever.

Brooklyn (Brook) Whitaker—Cassie's nine-year-old elder daughter. A shy girl who is slow to trust.

Jillian (Jilly) Whitaker—Cassie's seven-year-old, more outgoing younger child.

Dillon Diaz—Sergeant with the Jasper PD. Brady's best friend. Dillon is also a K-9 specialist.

Keith Norton—A successful dentist Cassie dated before moving back to Idaho.

Chapter One

Brady Nichols's date for the Daniels Canine Academy tenth-anniversary celebration party whined when he took the sharp curve a shade over the speed limit. They were late. He'd been running a full thirty minutes behind schedule the whole day, and his date was not inclined to be understanding.

So, he was rushing, and Brady hated rushing.

"We'll be there in a minute."

She didn't look at him. No, she simply sat there, staring through the glass with such intensity he was surprised she didn't cut a hole clean through the windshield.

Idaho wasn't as overrun as Oregon and Washington had become in recent years, but still, he'd moved to Jasper to get away from Boise and all the complications the city held. He wanted a quiet life. He'd purposefully chosen a location where he didn't have to be constantly vigilant, and he'd never regretted his choice. But his quiet life wasn't actually very quiet, and he was getting tired of taking flak from the needy blonde beside him.

He let off the gas as they navigated the next curve, and the Daniels ranch came into view. "See?" he prompted, nodding to a car signaling a turn into Emma Daniels's drive. He glanced at the clock on the dash, pleased to find he'd managed to recover about ten minutes. "Here we are."

He swerved to park in the spot on the lawn the young man wearing a yellow mesh safety vest indicated. He recognized the kid as one of the at-risk youths Emma routinely put to work at the DCA. Kevin? Kayson? No, Kyle. His name was Kyle.

Winnie let out a high-pitched whimper of excitement as he set the parking brake. Beside him, sixty-five pounds of pure happiness shivered with anticipation.

"There. We made it."

Winnie's sharp bark was one of pure joy, and he leaned over to pop the latch on the harness he used to keep her safely contained. His reward was a big, wet kiss. On the cheek, thankfully. Sometimes, in her exuberance, Winnie forgot they were partners first, friends second and the most significant being in one another's lives as a by-product of the first two.

He rubbed her silky ears, then looked her in the eyes as he stroked the dog's cheeks. It was a calming technique Emma had taught him when he first started working with the spirited yellow Lab. She'd been barely more than a pup with big paws, gangly legs and an eager-to-please attitude.

"Hold," he ordered, reaching for the door handle.

Winnie responded with another keening whimper of excitement, but stayed put. He climbed down from the truck and raised a hand to greet the young man in the vest. "Pulled parking duty, did ya?"

Kyle shrugged. "The safety vest is pretty lame, but it

beats emptying trash all night like William. And poor Hugh, he's the designated scooper," the kid informed him with a wrinkle of his nose. "I figure most everyone who's coming will be here in the next half hour or so."

"Good turnout?" Brady asked as he opened the passenger door.

Kyle motioned for an incoming minivan to park in the spot beside Brady's. "Yep. Tons of food too. People have been bringing stuff, even though Miss Emma told them not to."

Brady smirked. "People around here hate to come to parties empty-handed."

He ran a comforting hand down the dog's flank. Anticipation had her muscles quivering, but she made no move to exit the vehicle. She wouldn't until he gave her the go-ahead. He waited until he was certain the van was parked, then snapped his fingers.

Winnie barely gave him a chance to step out of the way. Her nose was pressed to the grass the minute she landed. She was trained from a pup to specialize in search and rescue, so Winnie's first instinct was to sniff to get her bearings.

"Lots of your friends here today, girl," he said, clipping her lead onto the vest she wore. Crouching beside her, he snapped twice, and she plopped her butt to the grass, her full attention on him. He framed her face again, stroking her smooth cheeks with his thumbs. "I'm sure you're psyched," he said in a low, even tone Emma had trained him to use when not giving actual commands. At two years old, Winnie still had a few puppy tendencies. They were working on smoothing out the rough edges together. "Hang with me until we get situated, then you can run with the pack, okay?"

She blinked, but her amber-brown gaze never wavered.

"Good girl," he said approvingly.

"Is he your doggy?"

The question came at him on a gasp of barely contained awe and delight.

Winnie's gaze darted past him and her tail thumped the ground hard enough to stir the dust. Brady twisted, still in his crouch, and found a girl with long blond pigtails gazing at them in slack-jawed wonder. He pressed his hands to his knees as he rose.

"Yes, *she* is. Her name is Winnie, and she is a proud graduate of Daniels Canine Academy. She's here for her homecoming."

Winnie's tail shifted from thump to full swoosh, and the girl beamed her approval. "Wow! She must be real smart. Mama says Miss Emma trains only the smartest, bestest dogs."

"Your mama is right," Brady replied, unable to resist returning her gap-toothed smile. "I'm Brady, and I'm a policeman here in Jasper. Winnie is my partner."

The girl's eyes widened to the size of quarters. "She's a police dog?"

"She sure is. Say hello, Winnie," he prompted, giving the yellow Lab's head a single pat. At the signal, Winnie let out a bark of greeting, then panted with excited expectation.

"Jillian?"

A woman's worried cry had all three of their heads whipping around. Seconds later, another slightly taller, but equally coltish girl appeared around the front of his truck. "She's right here, Mama," the girl called loudly. Then she eyed him with wary curiosity. "She's talking to a man."

Brady tightened his hold on Winnie's lead when a long, lanky woman with a mane of corn silk hair skidded to a stop beside the girls, an enormous purse dangling from her arm, and a covered dish clutched in both hands.

"Jilly, I've told you over and over you can't run off—"

"But he has a police dog. He's a policeman," Jillian replied like this was all the defense she needed. "I was only saying hi."

Brady aimed a cordial smile at the mother. She looked vaguely familiar, but he couldn't quite place her. "I'm Brady Nichols, ma'am. I'm with the Jasper PD." He glanced down at Winnie, who'd shifted closer to his leg, exerting the barest pressure to her lead. "This is Winnie. She's here to see some of her old classmates."

The woman blew out an exasperated breath, then tipped her head in his direction. "Nice to meet you, Officer Nichols. You too, Winnie," she added.

Her expression warmed as she shifted her attention to the dog, and Brady drew in a sharp breath. The woman was beautiful, but her looks weren't her most potent weapon. No, it was the pure pleasure he'd seen in her eyes when she found herself on the receiving end of Winnie's winning doggy grin.

He'd forever be a sucker for women who loved animals.

Glancing toward the large white tent erected between

the main house and the outbuildings, he said, "I'm glad I'm not the last to arrive."

"Oh no, we're chronically late," she said, her grimace wan.

Again, recognition niggled at him.

"I'm Jillian Marie Whitaker," the smaller girl volunteered. "Can I pet your doggy?"

"May I," her mother corrected.

Brady could tell by the well-rehearsed delivery this wasn't the first grammar lesson she'd given on the fly. "Sure," he said, bobbing a nod of assent. Jilly skittered forward, but he held out a hand to stop her. "Has anyone ever taught you how to approach a strange dog?"

She wagged her head so hard those long, silky pigtails whipped her face. "No," she replied. "I mean, no, sir," she adjusted, glancing over to her mother for approval.

Brady felt something in his gut loosen as he watched the silent exchange between mother and daughter. Turning his attention to the older girl, he motioned for her to join them. "Hi. I'm Brady. What's your name?"

"Brook," the girl answered shyly. Then, realizing her younger sister had set a more formal tone, she rolled her shoulders. "Brooklyn Ann Whitaker."

Matching her serious tone, he said, "Nice to meet you both. All," he amended almost immediately. He saw their mother shifting from foot to foot and readjusting the weight of the bag hanging off her arm. "But maybe we can put the lesson on hold for a minute. It looks like your mom might need a hand." He stretched both arms out and signaled for her to pass over the covered dish. "I'd be happy to carry something for you, ma'am."

"Her name is Mom, not ma'am," Jilly interjected helpfully.

"Her name is not Mom," Brook retorted. "Sheesh, don't you know anything?"

"Girls," their mother said in a warning tone. Returning her focus to him, she gave him a half-hearted flash of teeth. "I've got it, thank you. And my name is Cassie. Cassie Whitaker. And no, I'm not telling you my middle name."

The well-rehearsed intransigence in her tone coaxed a bark of laughter from him. "No?"

"She won't even tell us," Jilly said in a confidential tone. "It's a big secret."

"It's ridiculous and I hate it," Cassie said, shaking her hair away from her face. "Come on, girls. We can meet the doggies later. I don't want Aunt Vera to come looking for us."

At the mention of the name, the puzzle pieces snapped into place. "Aunt Vera? Oh! Vera from the diner. You're Millard's niece," he said. "I thought I'd seen you somewhere. You've been helping out at the diner, right?"

"Technically, Vera's niece, but yes, I've been trying to help out here and there." The screech of a public address system coming to life yanked their attention to the tent, and worry puckered her brow. "I have to get this over there."

"You heard the lady, Winnie. Stop distracting these pretty girls."

He watched as Cassie Whitaker strode ahead, her gaze fixed on the crowd wandering in from all directions. Brook hurried after her mother, but Jilly appeared reluctant to leave Winnie's side. The stubborn set of her mouth spoke volumes about the rebellions she'd launch in the future, but for now, he wasn't willing to get tangled in one. He liked his life easy and uncomplicated, and a pretty woman with two precocious children were three complications too many.

"Go on now," he urged his new friend. "You get us in trouble with your mama, she'll never let Winnie run with the likes of you."

She must have enjoyed the notion of getting a grown man in trouble because she aimed her sunbeam grin at him again. "You think Winnie will let me run with her?"

"Definitely. You get on with your mama. Find us after dinner. I hear Miss Emma has a special obstacle course set up. That's where we'll be."

With a soft "Yay!" she gave Winnie a pat goodbye, then skipped ahead to catch her mother and sister.

Brady forced himself to tear his gaze from Cassie Whitaker's long, tanned legs, but it wasn't easy. The white denim shorts were more flattering than the T-shirt and jeans she covered with an apron when working at Millard's Diner.

Once they disappeared into the shadows of the tent, he steered Winnie toward the far end where he saw a few of his colleagues and Winnie's fellow DCA alums congregated. At his approach, his best friend, Dillon, raised his can of beer in salute.

"You came," Dillon said, gruff but sounding pleased.

Brady felt a blush prickle his cheeks but hoped his beard masked it. He wasn't a fan of the spotlight, no matter how small the circle. He rarely attended these town shindigs, mainly because he wasn't particularly adept at small talk, and so it was hard to imagine anyone would have missed his absence on this occasion.

"I did. The boss insisted," he added, nodding to the dog at his side. Winnie and Dillon's dog, Bentley, a spirited Australian shepherd mix, exchanged sniffs in greeting.

"Do you good to get out. Mix and mingle a bit." Dillon gestured to Brady's face, then rubbed his own cheek. "Starting to look gristly in your off-hours."

"And since these are my off-hours, I don't need any commentary from you," Brady retorted.

"Saw you walking with Cassie from the diner," Dillon said. "Cute girls."

The switch in subjects was so abrupt, Brady gave his head a shake to settle the pieces into place. "Oh yeah. I didn't recognize her at first."

Dillon smirked. "Because you hardly look up from your plate whenever we're in there. You really need to learn how to cook for yourself."

"I can cook," Brady argued. "But I don't see the point in making a mess when it's only me. I have better things to do."

"Speaking of your to-do list, do you still need a hand tomorrow?" his best friend asked.

"Yeah, if you don't mind," Brady confirmed. He was starting to frame the interior walls on the house he was building, and though he'd devised an elaborate system of clamping and positioning lumber by himself, the task went much faster when there was a second pair of hands on the job.

"No problem, but I only accept cash, credit or pizza and beer. No personal checks."

"Pizza and beer it is," Brady confirmed.

The words had barely left his mouth when Barbara Macy, the woman who kept all the balls in the air for the Daniels Canine Academy, stepped to the mic. There was a sharp burst of static, then the piercing screech of feedback as she removed the microphone from its holder. The crowd let out a collective groan, and at his side, Winnie concurred with a soft keening sound.

Barbara spoke into the mic. "I keep telling Emma a live mic is better than a dog whistle, but I still can't get her to karaoke night at the Bart."

Brady chuckled with the rest of the crowd. Bartwell Brewing Company had purchased a karaoke setup complete with flashing lights and two microphones for duets, but few of the town's residents had been brave enough to jump onto the ministage.

"Thank you all for coming out," she said, beaming at the crowd. "Em said she didn't want a lot of fuss, but I think ten years of hard work, perseverance and excellence are worth celebrating, don't you?"

The crowd clapped heartily, and a few whistles, shout-outs and barks punctuated the applause.

She gestured to the tables overflowing with food and gave her head a rueful shake. "I could've sworn the invitation said food would be provided. I hope you all brought some plastic tubs to haul all this home. You know Emma is adamant about not feeding table scraps to the dogs."

"I'll take the leftovers," Jason Wright, the rookie on the Jasper PD squad and one of Emma's foster sons, called out. A few other men in the crowd were quick to volunteer their help as well, including chief of police, Doug Walters.

Ahead of them, Maisy Barton announced, "I brought zipper bags and plastic margarine tubs. A whole box of them!" Then she nudged her teenage granddaughter, who looked like she was hoping the ground would open and swallow her. "See? I told you people would want them."

Brady ducked his head and his mouth watered. He'd make sure he was in line for some of those leftovers. He was tired of microwave pizza pastries when he wasn't eating at the diner.

"I've asked the woman of the hour to say a few words, but in typical Emma fashion, she keeps trying to refuse."

Barbara gestured to Emma Daniels, who shook her head in stubborn refusal. Brady cringed inwardly as the assembled crowd called out encouragement, and Emma's face colored. He felt for the woman he'd come to consider a friend. Mortification was ten times worse when a person was shoved into the limelight.

Brady thought Emma might actually turn and walk straight out of the tent, but then Tashya Pratt leaned over and spoke directly into her foster mother's ear. Barbara continued to cajole Emma, although Brady could tell the trainer's focus had shifted entirely to the pretty young vet tech who'd returned home to work by her side.

He saw Emma mouth the word *Seriously?* as her brows reached for the sky.

Tashya beamed, then waved in their direction, gesturing for someone to join her. Brady saw Jason shouldering his way through the crowd toward the girl he'd loved since they were teenagers, his joyous expression a match for Tashya's, and now Emma's.

"Something's going on there," Dillon murmured.

Brady couldn't disagree. The crowd grew restless, murmuring to each other as Barbara's efforts to get Emma to say a few words appeared to be thwarted. But then Emma strode straight toward the PA system.

Barbara jumped when Emma practically yanked the mic from her hand.

"Thank you all for coming out," she said, her words booming through the speaker, her shout amplified enough to make several of the dogs in attendance plant their behinds firmly on the ground.

Brady chuckled when Winnie's rear landed on his foot. She clearly didn't care; her gaze, along with almost everyone else's, was pinned on the woman who'd been his dog's first love.

"Sorry," Emma said with a grimace. She gestured for Jason and Tashya to join her. "I do appreciate you all coming. I consider you all family, even if some of you only have two legs." The crowd chuckled, well aware she wasn't completely joking. "My whole life, you've all been so supportive. Of me, of my dogs, of the kids we've all tried to help over the years. This party is to celebrate life. Our lives, the lives of the dogs and of those we love." She glanced over at Tashya, silently asking for her consent, and the younger woman waved eager permission to proceed. "But I'm thrilled to tell you we have something more exciting than an anniversary to celebrate. Today, we get to share in a new beginning.

So, lift your glasses and fill your plates. Jason finally put a ring on my girl Tashya's finger!"

The younger woman held her left hand high and waggled her fingers, showing off a ring so tiny Brady could barely see it from where he stood.

Beside him, Dillon groaned. "Engaged? Another one bites the dust."

Brady shot his buddy a worried glance, then returned his attention to the woman with the microphone. "To Jason and Tashya." Emma lifted her glass to toast the engaged couple, and others did the same. "I'm so happy I don't have to ground either of you for sneaking around anymore."

Chapter Two

Two hours later, Brady had his elbows braced on the top of a split-rail fence and a cold can of beer in his hand. He was feeling about as content as a man could get. His belly was full, he had his best pal by his side and his best girl was running around with a bunch of other dogs, showing her impressive skills.

Behind him, the tent glowed with strings of lights. He figured they were Barbara's doing. He couldn't imagine Emma even considering such a thing. She would have been too busy thinking about the training hours she was losing with the dogs.

Still, she seemed to be enjoying the party almost as much as everyone else was. Brady himself had eaten a heaping plate of barbecue, then gone for seconds, sampling a spoonful of most everything else, including all the desserts. There was nothing like a potluck to test a man's endurance. He was pretty sure he'd made a good showing.

Dillon leaned against the fence too. Brady had noted his friend was outpacing him two to one on the beers, but for the most part, Dillon seemed to be holding his own. Still, Brady worried. "You doin' okay, bud?"

Dillon hummed, his gaze fixed on the horizon where the mountains rose abruptly out of the patch of prairie the Daniels family had claimed long ago. "A OK," he replied.

But his tone held a sarcastic edge. He wasn't fooling anyone, much less his best friend. Dillon was all torn up over some woman named Rosie he'd met on a ski weekend.

"You've got to let it go, man," Brady said quietly. "Thinking about her is eating you up inside. You've got to let her go."

"Pffft," Dillon hissed. "Let her go? She's gone. I let her go."

"I mean, let the idea of her go," Brady persisted.

"The idea of her," Dillon echoed. "You been reading self-help books?"

The disdain in his friend's tone stung, but Brady kept his expression impassive as he stood beside the other man staring at the horizon. "Nah. I try not to read too much. My lips get too tired."

Dillon snorted a laugh, and both men fell quiet as they refocused on the action in the fenced arena. Their dogs and a couple dozen others ran through the obstacle course the DCA staff had laid out for them with joyous abandon. The enclosure was rife with lolling pink tongues, damp noses and wagging tails. As always, there'd been some growling and nipping as a new pack order was established, but no serious altercations.

The same could not be said for the impromptu game of softball the adults were playing in another part of the yard. At least the kids seemed to be content. A bunch of them were still lining up to play the yard games organized by the staff. Ring toss, bean bag throwing and a lawn bowling set complete with plastic pins and a foam ball.

A mix of adults and children stood along the fence separating humans from the dogs, watching the animals run the course and calling out encouragement to their favorites. Occasionally, he checked to make sure Winnie was playing well with the others. But his attention kept drifting to Dillon's somber quietness. He was trying to think of what to say next, what advice he could mine from the disintegration of his marriage to give his friend, but though he'd moved away from Boise and started a new life here in Jasper, he was no glowing example of moving on.

Sure, he had a new job and a new dog, and soon he'd have walls in his new house, but he was still another divorced police officer trying to scratch out a fresh start. He lived in a double-wide and ate pastry pizzas fresh from the microwave. He was certainly not the guy to give out handfuls of unsolicited advice.

A commotion over in the children's game area drew his attention. Cassie Whitaker seemed to be moving from one game to the next, questioning the children at each station. His focus had snagged on her more than a few times since they arrived. He couldn't help it; she looked so different than she did when she was working at the diner. Freer. Less frenzied and more…arresting. She had a fresh-faced, girl-next-door look, but moved with such assurance, no one would dare mistake her for anything but a grown woman who knew who she was.

Until now.

Now, she looked frantic.

Instinctively, he straightened to his full height when she spun away from the games area and set off toward the enclosure where he stood. But she wasn't looking at him. He watched, concern prickling his neck as she scanned the people lined along the fence. Then he realized her girls weren't with her.

"Something's happening," he said, nudging Dillon, then nodding toward the leggy blonde.

Dillon rolled his shoulders and lowered the can of beer to his side. Brady was glad to see his friend was steady on his feet, despite the beers he'd downed.

Cassie stopped at a cluster of people gathered at the opposite side of the ring, but whatever she'd asked, the answer had been nothing but head shakes and concerned frowns. She moved in their direction, and Brady started toward her, drawn like steel to a magnet.

There was trouble.

She was troubled.

And he didn't like seeing her pretty face creased with worry.

He didn't examine those reactions too closely. Instead, he followed his instinct and let his feet carry him to her side. He paused beside the group of people she'd stopped to question and overheard her describing her two girls to them. In detail. Right down to the color of the elastic bands holding their hair in pigtails. Cassie twisted her fingers into knots when she was met with yet more negative responses and expressions of concern. His gut tightened.

"What's wrong? Did something happen to one of the girls?" he demanded, blocking her path to the next group of people at the fence.

"Oh. It's you." She looked at him like he was a genie who'd appeared from a magic bottle. Then she clutched his arm. "Wait. You said you're a police officer, right? What was your name? Brendan?"

"Brady, ma'am," he corrected, refusing to acknowledge the sting of being so forgettable to this woman. "Lieutenant Brady Nichols with the Jasper PD."

"I'm sorry. Brady. Brady," she repeated trying to get it to sink in even as she looked past his shoulder to scan the area around them. Her gaze returned to his. She was twitchy. Distressed. "I can't find my girls. I've looked everywhere," she said, panic making her voice slide into a higher register. "Everywhere." She shook her head hard in frustration, then brushed a strand of hair stuck to the corner of her mouth away impatiently. "I told them they could go play games, but not to go anywhere else. I've asked everyone working the games, but no one's seen them."

Brady took her arm. "I'll help you look for them." He jerked a thumb at Dillon, who had followed close behind him. "This is Dillon. He's with the JPD as well." He looked at his friend. "We're looking for two girls, ages—"

"Nine and seven," Cassie provided.

Dillon immediately pulled out his phone and began typing a note. "Two girls, ages nine and seven," he repeated. "Names?"

"Brooklyn and Jillian," Cassie provided. "Brook is nine. She was supposed to keep an eye on Jilly."

"I'm sure she is," Brady assured her. Turning to Dillon, he said, "Both blonde. Both wearing their hair in two long, uh…" He gestured to the sides of his own head, then pulled his hands downward to indicate long hair.

"Pigtails," she supplied the word, though it came out watery.

Brady peered down at her, his heart flipping over at the sight of tears pooling in her eyes. He tamped down the urge to comfort her and kept his expression carefully blank as he focused on getting the pertinent information. "Can you repeat what they were wearing?" Brady asked, keeping his tone gentle. "Jillian had something pink on, right?" He wanted to kick himself for not paying closer attention to her kid.

"Yes," Cassie said eagerly. "Both girls are wearing white shorts and short-sleeve tops. Brooklyn's is blue with a unicorn on it, and Jilly's is pink with a glittery puppy dog." She turned big hazel eyes to Brady, her expression a plea for understanding. "She's been wanting a dog forever, and I… It's a lot having the two of them on my own. I can't imagine a dog. It's one of the reasons I told Aunt Vera we'd come today. I wanted to give her the chance to meet the dogs," she finished with a shrug.

Brady placed a gentle hand on her shoulder, hoping to give some comfort. "I'm sure Winnie enjoyed meeting her. And she couldn't have picked a better dog to meet first because she's Officer Winnie, a trained search and rescue dog. Whenever we have hikers get too far off the trails—" he pointed to the woods leading into the foothills of the mountains "—Winnie goes and finds them and brings them home safe."

She raised a horrified hand to her mouth, and Brady quickly pivoted away from the possibility of a search. "But I don't think we need a full search. I saw a bunch of kids hanging out around the dessert table, snitching cookies and poking their fingers into the whipped cream on the pies. Why don't you go check there while Dillon and I ask around a bit? They may have gone to the tent to find you," he suggested.

Cassie's head whipped toward the tent, and she pressed a hand flat against her chest. "Brook does have a sweet tooth," she said hoarsely. "She'd eat nothing but candy and cookies all day long if I let her."

Brady let his hand fall to his side. "But I'm sure you don't let her." Her gaze flew to his, and he shrugged. "You seem like a good mom. The kind who makes her kids eat vegetables and gets all the tangles out of their hair at bedtime. I can't imagine it's an easy job, so cut yourself some slack. And once we find them, we'll make sure to tell them they can visit Winnie or Dillon's dog, Bentley, whenever they're downtown. The dogs are always happy to meet with members of the public."

Dillon scoped the area. "I'm gonna start over at the softball game and see if anyone's seen them, then I'll circle around this way. Brady, you cover the dogs and the kids' games again while their mama checks the dessert table." He switched his attention to Brady. "They couldn't have gone far without someone noticing them wandering away. Not out here."

Brady watched as Cassie hurried to the tent, no doubt hoping to find her girls sneaking treats at one of the rapidly emptying tables. When Brady met Dillon's worried gaze, he found his friend's mouth set in a grim line. "You don't think they're eating dessert," he stated flatly.

"Who knows?" Dillon shrugged. "I hope so, but

there are so many people here. It's hard to weed through them all."

Brady gave a nod. Not too long ago he'd been the new guy in town, eyed with suspicion and greeted with wariness for months after he'd made the move to Jasper. Emma Daniels trained dogs for police departments and federal agencies. She dealt with people who reached far beyond the insular circle of Jasper, Idaho. There had indeed been many people who were not locals attending the festivities.

"I get you. Let's move on this," Brady said brusquely. Placing two fingers between his lips, he whistled sharply. Winnie stopped frolicking with the German shepherd she'd chosen as her playmate. He whistled two more short bursts, and she ran to the rail where he stood. "Come," he said quietly, and she shimmied out beneath the bottom rail of the fence.

Despite his worry, he chuckled at the dog's single-minded determination. "You could have used the gate." Pulling the looped lead from the post beside him, he clipped it to her harness.

Dillon stepped to the fence and shouted, "Bentley, come!" The Australian shepherd immediately abandoned the Frisbee he'd been carrying in his mouth and dashed toward Dillon.

With their dogs by their sides, the two men took off in different directions. Brady paused long enough to glance at the tent and saw Cassie moving from table to table asking the occupants nearby if they'd seen her girls, and bending to peek beneath each one.

He covered the remainder of the spectators watching the dogs and went to the area where the children's games were arranged. At the bean bag station, Piper Lambert, one of the DCA staff who'd helped train Winnie, shook her head sadly. "No, I told Cassie I haven't seen them. I hope she finds them soon. It's so worrisome when they wander away," she said, a frown puckering her brow.

Then a boy who had been inching closer to Winnie shook his head. "They didn't wander away," he said. "Their daddy came and took 'em for a walk. They went thataway." He extended a hand to point to the mountains darkening in the rapidly falling dusk.

Chapter Three

"No. No, no, no, no, no," Cassie Whitaker said adamantly.

"No, it wasn't your husband?" Brady asked, hoping to stop the trembling woman in front of him from shaking her head so hard. He was almost afraid she'd concuss herself.

Behind him, Dillon mumbled, "I'm going with no."

"He's not my husband anymore," Cassie asserted brusquely. "He doesn't even live around here. He lives in Billings, Montana. There's no way he came here. I'm not even sure he has a clue where we are."

Brady's brow creased. "He doesn't have any kind of visitation arrangement with the children?"

"No."

"She's batting a thousand with the noes," Dillon murmured.

Casting a quelling glance over his shoulder, Brady said, "What's your ex-husband's name? Can you give us an address or phone number? A description? Anything you can think of off the top of your head would help. Dillon can make himself useful by trying to run him to ground," he said, cocking an eyebrow at his friend.

Brady slapped the grip on Winnie's lead against his thigh as Cassie rattled off the information. When she was done, he cast another glance out at the rapidly darkening sky and said, "Do you have any clothes the girls might have worn today? You said something about sweatshirts. Do you have their sweatshirts here?"

The urgency in his tone must have registered for her because she strode quickly to one of the few remaining tables still set up in the tent. He watched as she pulled a tangled wad of clothing from the enormous tote bag he'd seen swinging from her arm earlier. Emma and some of the Daniels Academy folks followed in her wake.

"Jilly's is clean, but Brook tends to run cold. She had hers on in the car earlier. She doesn't like the air-conditioning blowing on her."

Brady waggled his finger between the two sweat-shirts, then chose the slightly larger one. "This one?"

Cassie bit her lip. "Yes. Oh, Brookie," she said in a husky whisper. "She'll be cold."

Brady took the sweatshirt from her. Turning to Barbara and Emma, he said, "It's getting dark, but I think Winnie and I can take a quick walk across the field to see if we can find any scent."

Emma Daniels agreed with a brusque nod. "Is your phone charged? Do you need a flashlight?" she asked without further conversation.

Brady touched the phone case clipped to his belt. "Yes, ma'am, and no. Thank you," he added as an afterthought. "I'll be right back."

He led Winnie from the tent out into the open pasture between them and the wooded foothills of the mountains. Once they were away from the circle of lights, he stood and waited until their eyes adjusted. Then he leaned down and held the small soft sweatshirt out for Winnie to sniff.

"Here, girl. Remember your friends from earlier? We've gotta go find them."

He spoke in a hushed but commanding tone he knew the Lab responded to best. Obediently, Winnie went to work, snuffling around in the folds of the fabric until her muscles tightened and her fur rippled with anticipation.

"You got 'em?" he asked the dog.

Her floppy ears twitched forward and her brow wrinkled. She strained against the lead ever so slightly, but didn't move. Smiling, he gave her head a pat, unlatched the lock on the retractable lead and said, "Let's go find them."

The two of them took off across the field covered in stubbly grass at a jog. Two minutes in, the retractable leash had stretched as far as it could. She far outpaced him with her four-legs-to-two advantage.

If it weren't so close to dark, he might have let her off the leash, but while she was well trained, she was also still young and stubborn. Sometimes, Winnie had a mind of her own and hadn't quite learned how to obey an order she didn't agree with. He couldn't risk losing her to the dark as well.

The grass gave way to brush, then brush thickened to include sapling trees that stood as tall as he did. Their pace slowed markedly. Winnie paused to sniff various points in the undergrowth, and he took in some of the slack on the retractable leash. Under the cover of trees, the darkness started to close in around them more rapidly. Fearing they might not be able to pick up a trace, Brady shortened the distance between himself and Winnie until they stood side by side again.

Through the darkening gloom, he could see the dog's worried frown. He stroked her head reassuringly. "It's not you. You're doing great."

She needed only those few words of reassurance. Winnie pressed her nose to the ground again and started working the area around where he stood in a small circle. He gave her as much leeway as the clearing would allow, but soon he'd have to call it quits for the night. Hopefully, whoever the girls had left with had taken them into town, and one of the people combing the streets of Jasper would be sure to spot them.

He was about to signal for Winnie to call off the hunt when the dog went stock-still. Brady froze as well, barely daring to breathe. He waited patiently, certain she would not act until her olfactory senses told her she had something real. Within seconds, she lifted her head, her ears perked and she lunged forward, leading him off to his left.

Brady jogged through the scrub, branches hitting him in the face as he struggled to release the clasp on the lead. Once she was free, he followed her through the thickening trees as close as he could, hanging back enough to keep her in sight but not distracting her from her primary focus. They'd gone about a hundred yards when she let out a low woof to warn him she was about to take off in earnest.

Brady quickened his pace, his heart rate accelerating at the possibility of locating the girls. Panting, he jumped over a fallen log and thrashed at protruding limbs as he ran, heedless of the scratches forming on his forearms.

But then, Winnie gave another bark, this one shorter and sharper. A bark of frustration.

He was so fixated on following the direction of her call in the new all-encompassing dark, he hadn't registered the clearing he approached until he stumbled out of the woods onto a dirt road, tripping on an exposed root as he burst forth. Winnie barked again as he fell to the hard-packed dirt and gravel. He muttered a curse in response.

Mere yards away, his dog circled an area near the side of the road. Rolling to his knees, Brady tapped the flashlight icon on his phone and surveyed the area. It appeared to be one of the many gravel and dirt tracks cut by the forestry service over the years. This particular one seemed to have fallen down a few notches on the maintenance list. He pushed to his feet and dusted the dirt from his jeans as he walked toward the circling dog. At his approach, Winnie sighed and looked at him, her brow furrowed. A high, keening whine escaped her.

He reached down and gave her head a consoling pat. If Winnie was giving up, the trail had gone truly cold. He held his phone high to take in the area once more, then directed the flashlight at the road.

Tire tracks heading into the hills.

Whoever had taken Cassie Whitaker's girls had driven. On foot, they could be anywhere, but roads were rough and limited in the foothills. They wouldn't make it far. He saw no signs of a turnaround. No flattened scrub or crumpled saplings on either side of the narrow lane. It was possible whoever it was had taken the road higher into the mountains, but most of these roads only led as far as forestry service outposts. He'd have to get the records from town to find out where this particular lane would dead-end.

He'd have to wait until morning to look for better clues.

The dog whimpered again, and Brady dropped to her side. Stroking her cheeks, he looked directly into those amber eyes and spoke calmly. "Good girl. You are a good girl. Good work." He rubbed her head once more, then clipped the lead to her harness. "Come on. We'll head downtown and see what we can figure out tonight, but I promise, you'll be on the case tomorrow. You're gonna need a good night's rest."

The dog resisted enough to show she was as dissatisfied with the result as he was, but followed obediently. The walk to the Daniels ranch seemed to go much faster than the climb into the mountains, even though he had to use the more circuitous route along the road. Dread pooled low in his belly. He returned from searches empty-handed all too often, but he'd never grown immune to the looks of profound disappointment on loved ones' faces when they saw him and Winnie returning alone.

The lights under the tent had been shut off, but every lamp in the old ranch house was ablaze. There were also at least a dozen cars parked close, including three Jasper PD units. As he circled around the pasture to the front of the house, Brady cast a glance at the far field where two vehicles sat abandoned—his truck and Cassie Whitaker's minivan.

He approached the building, his stomach twisting

into a knot. He'd barely climbed the first step when she spoke from a dark corner of the porch.

"No luck?" Cassie Whitaker asked, the question tremulous.

Since he wasn't returning with two blondes on his arms, Brady saw no point in soft selling his failure. "No, ma'am, but I promise you, Winnie and I are gonna be out first thing in the morning." He took a step closer, squinting to make out her features in the dim light emanating from the house. "You shouldn't be out here alone."

"Too many people in there, and none of them the ones I want to see," she returned.

He made a grunt of understanding. "We did pick up their scent crossing the field and into the woods."

She let out a strangled "Oof," but managed to suck it in quickly. "You think whoever it was took them into the woods?"

"Maybe. It's only a guess," he hastened to add. "The trail went cold at one of the fire lanes. Most likely, whoever they're with had a vehicle parked there. We have to remember they could be holed up somewhere in town," he said, extending a dim ray of hope.

The corner of her mouth curved down, and she shook her head sadly. "They're not in town. Your boss is in there talking to Emma right now. They've looked everywhere and no one's seen them."

"Yet," he added. "Doesn't mean no one will," Brady reminded her. "I think the good news is whoever they're with is somebody they know. Hopefully somebody they trust. No one saw them struggle or heard them yelling or crying, so I think this may be the case. Hopefully, they are with someone who won't hurt them."

"You'd think," she muttered, a bitter note in her tone. "But we don't know many people here yet, aside from Aunt Vera and Uncle Millard."

"If you don't mind, I'd like to go into the station. Dillon's working on tracking down your ex, and we'll have better access to resources there." He glanced over at the brightly lit house. "I'd say we shouldn't impose on Emma any further, but she'll be doing everything she can to help find them. Everyone will be," he asserted. "Jasper is a small town, and they take care of their own."

"I'm not sure we're one of their own yet," Cassie replied huskily.

"You are. Your grandparents lived here, right? Your mother and aunt grew up here. Vera may not be a ray of sunshine, but people still love her." He gestured for her to rise. "I'll give them the heads-up we're leaving. You can either ride with me or follow me downtown."

After a flurry of goodbyes and reassurances from the people still hanging around the Daniels ranch, including the chief himself, they walked across the darkened field. The grass lay flat, the only proof it had been the parking area hours earlier. The moon was high and bright now, but not quite bright enough to search. The night breeze cut through his T-shirt. Those girls would be cold, and the worry sat like a lump of ice in his gut.

Winnie trotted at his side, off her leash since it was the three of them alone. As they approached the vehicles, Cassie spoke.

"Thank you for doing this," she said earnestly. "I

wasn't… I wasn't particularly friendly earlier," she said, glancing over at his truck.

The light from the moon was enough to outline the worry and regret etched into her pretty face. "You were fine," he said firmly. "I wouldn't expect any parent to take too kindly to their kid talking to a strange man."

The corners of her mouth sloped down. "I've been talking to Jilly about stranger danger," she said with a short, bitter laugh. "I guess those lessons haven't stuck."

Unable to refrain any longer, Brady reached out and placed a hand on her shoulder. When she jolted, he gave it a gentle squeeze and withdrew, signaling he meant the gesture as nothing more than a comfort.

"I'd tell you not to worry, but that would be futile," he said with a self-deprecating chuckle. "If you weren't worried, I'd think there was something wrong with you."

She absorbed his assertion. "Would you take me to the spot where…?"

She didn't say "where you lost them," but he felt the unspoken words like a gut punch. Drawing in a sharp breath, he inclined his head, even though the thought tied his stomach into a knot.

He gestured to her minivan. "Sure. Why don't you ride with us, then we'll get your car and head into town?"

"Okay." She ducked her head and made her way to the passenger side of his truck. He reached for the handle and opened the door, but she didn't climb in. Instead, her gazed was fixed on the harness he used for Winnie. "Should I get in the back?"

"Oh. No, sorry." He unhooked the harness and tossed it in. Opening the half door to the rear seat, he said, "Winnie, up."

The dog obeyed without hesitation. Once she was settled, her muzzle resting on her paws, Brady gave her a pat and murmured, "There you go. Good girl." He closed the rear door, then gestured to the vacant seat. "Help yourself."

"What? You don't want to order me to jump?" she asked as she grabbed the handle above the door and stepped into the truck.

Happy to hear a touch of sass in her tone, Brady stood in the open passenger door as she reached for the safety belt and then clipped it in place. She raised her eyebrows and he smirked. "There you are. Good girl." He gave the roof a pat, then closed the door on her husky chuckle.

Chapter Four

Cassie had spent a couple weeks with her grandparents in Jasper almost every summer of her childhood, but she never strayed too far from town. As an adult, she'd gone down many an unpaved road leading to hiking trails and points of river access, but she'd never had a chance to follow this particular road. The gravel lane was so rutted, they bounced around in the cab, trying to maintain equilibrium. She was glad she hadn't tried to drive her minivan. Poor old thing would never have made it.

They'd ridden in silence, but it wasn't the uncomfortable kind. It was sort of…full.

Full of worry. Full of wondering. Full of concern.

She could feel the frustration practically rolling off both the man beside her and the dog behind them. They clearly wanted to act. Cassie was so appreciative of their determination she was tempted to cry. But she wouldn't. Couldn't. She didn't have time for an emotional breakdown. As a mother, she was an absolute expert on shoving her own feelings aside in order to focus on what needed to be done.

Until she'd moved to Jasper, no one cared about her girls the way she did. Certainly not their father.

"It wasn't Mark," she said, her words low and throaty, as she watched the scrubby brush zoom past her window.

A bitter laugh escaped her, but there was no point in trying to sugarcoat anything. Brady and his friend Dillon would find out exactly how useless her ex-husband was in due course.

"He has a drinking problem. It pretty much consumes him. He hasn't tried to see the girls once since we left. I can't imagine him going to this extreme. Too much effort," she concluded, chancing a glance at the man beside her.

He gave a short nod. "I'm sorry," he said gruffly. "It must have been rough on you and the girls."

"Actually, leaving Mark was one of the easiest things I've ever done," she said simply. She didn't wait for any follow-up questions he might have.

"After the divorce we moved to Bozeman." She gazed out the window again, though the shapes beyond the glass grew more and more indistinct in the deepening dark. "I actually liked the life I built in Bozeman. I had a good job and a nice apartment," she said her, tone tremulous. She swallowed hard. "I'd even started dating again. Talk about a mistake."

"Mistake?" Brady asked as he let off the accelerator and the truck rolled to a halt on the steadily rising incline. She waited until he set the brake to speak.

"I'm concerned one of the men I dated in Bozeman might be behind this," she said, letting the words form as the idea took shape in her mind. "I'd hoped he'd lose interest if I didn't answer anymore, but…"

"But he didn't," he prompted when she trailed off.

"No," she replied, not offering anything more.

"What makes you think it might be this guy? What's his name?" he asked, the questions coming at her faster than she anticipated.

"Keith," she supplied. "Keith Norton. As for the why, it was a messy sort of breakup."

"Messy how?" Brady asked.

"I could see it wasn't going to be a long-term thing for us, so I ended it." She clamped her mouth shut, unsure how much more she wanted to share. After all, she had no real reason to suspect Keith other than his persistence.

Brady reached over and touched her forearm with two fingers. The movement was purposefully nonthreatening. Nothing more than a means of getting her attention. Still, she couldn't look directly at him. She stared straight ahead through the windshield at the narrow red dirt-and-gravel road illuminated by the truck's headlights.

"Is this it?" she asked, hating the break in her voice but unable to muster the strength to hold it together.

"Hard to say exactly in the dark," Brady said. "I figured we'd get out of here and let Winnie have a sniff around."

Cassie waited impatiently for him to get down to it. At last, he snatched something from the center console and reached for the handle on the door. She watched as Brady rummaged under the seat of the truck and pulled out a heavy-duty flashlight. He clicked it on and off, checking to be sure the batteries were still strong. Then he opened the door on his side of the truck, and Winnie jumped down to stand by his side.

"I'm going to leave her off lead, if you don't mind," he informed her.

Cassie shook her head hard. "Are you kidding? She could do whatever she wants as far as I'm concerned."

Warmed by her appreciation for Winnie's skill, he patted the dog's head. "But won't," he said, shifting his attention to his partner.

Cassie watched as he dropped to a crouched position and spoke directly to the dog. It reminded her of the way she spoke to Jilly. Focused. One-on-one.

He stroked Winnie's face as he talked, his cadence and demeanor gentle but firm. "Right, girl? I need you to stay on track, okay?" he murmured to the dog.

Cassie's heart leaped into her throat when she saw him offer Brook's sweatshirt to the dog to sniff. The Lab's ears thrust forward and her poor head wrinkled. She kept snuffling as Brady rose to his feet, and gave her a pat on the head. "Go on. Search," he prompted.

Standing by the front bumper of the truck, Cassie watched the dog press her nose to the dirt and start working the area. If it weren't her girls they were searching for, Cassie would have been more fascinated by the process and the dog's methodology, but her girls were missing, and it was hard for Cassie to do anything but stare into the darkened woods surrounding them.

"She's good." The compliment came out rusty, but she needed to say something. The chirp of crickets surrounding them was becoming unbearable.

Brady cast a sidelong glance at her. "She was almost a DCA washout," he informed her. "Emma was having a hard time finding someone who could connect with her in a way Winnie responded to positively. She was still a puppy and a bit all over the place."

"And the two of you connected?"

"Yep." He chuckled. "I never considered myself a dog person. Didn't have one growing up. Didn't work K-9 when I was on the force in Boise, but when I met Winnie…it was all over."

Cassie kept her eyes fixed on the Labrador caught in the headlight beams. The dog kept her nose to the ground, looking determined. She moved about five more feet along the lane, then stopped, lifted her head and let out a soft woof. Brady moved toward her. "There's the spot. She lost the scent there," he informed Cassie.

She hurried behind him. "Where does this road lead?"

"It's a fire lane. There is a whole maze of them, most overgrown, but interconnected. They usually lead to a ranger station or a fire lookout. We'll have to get the maps out when we get down to the station."

She watched as he pulled out his cell phone and opened a mapping application, dropping a pin in the spot where they stood. When he swiveled the screen to her, she saw their location coordinates displayed in the message box. He'd literally marked the spot.

Cassie turned in a slow circle, narrowing her eyes as she peered into the ever-deepening darkness beyond the headlight's beams. Logically, she knew there was no point in them trying to go on tonight, but logic wasn't playing a big part in her way of thinking right now.

Reading her thoughts, Brady placed a gentle hand on her shoulder. "The best thing we can do is go down to the station, do some research and prepare for the morning. I promise you we will be out at first light."

The sincerity in his tone made her swallow hard. "I understand," she croaked. "I'm sure you're right, but…"

"You're anxious. Believe me, if it made any sense for us to get out there right now, we would. We'll go down to the station and see if there's any new information."

"If you don't mind taking me to my car, I'll follow you," she said. "I want to have my car."

He bobbed his head once. "You think you're all right to drive?"

"Yeah," she said briefly, then yanked open the passenger door.

Brady watched as she strapped herself into the seat. Winnie barked and Cassie was not surprised when he kicked it into gear. Once Brady had Winnie loaded into her harness, Cassie gave the dog a pat. "Thank you."

Winnie replied with a low hum of a growl.

Clearly, the dog was as frustrated as she and Brady.

He glanced over his shoulder after he executed a tight three-point turn on the narrow lane. "We're going to find them, right, girl?" Winnie turned her head to look at the woods where they'd lost the scent. "First thing tomorrow, I promise."

Cassie waved, but she had no doubt her expression was as somber as Winnie's.

Chapter Five

Brady's eyes kept flicking to the rearview mirror, and his mind raced as he led Cassie into Jasper. The woman was clearly in shock. But rather than crumpling under the weight of what was happening, she seemed to grow more…steely.

He figured it had to do with being a single parent. Every single mom or dad he knew had this miles-deep well of calm they could draw on in times of extreme stress. It fascinated him. He never thought he was much of a kid guy himself, but he had friends, and a few had become parents. He was glad he and Lisa never had kids. Their divorce had been messy enough all on its own. Dragging innocent children into the mix would have made it worse.

Lisa hadn't been the type to settle down once the wedding was over. Oh, she loved the whole white dress and rigamarole. All the attention. But settling into married life? She chafed against it from the beginning. Resented the days when his work hours ate into what she considered their time. Hated the danger inherent in his job even though he had been a cop when they'd met.

He understood how hard it was on the spouses, so

he listened to her complaints with as much patience as he could muster, but after a while he realized her grievances with his career choices had nothing do with his safety and more to do with their lifestyle.

Lisa had been five years younger. She wasn't done with her partying. Other than shopping for home decor, she wasn't much interested in anything domestic. He never expected her to turn into a television housewife, but it would have been nice to have a meal prepared occasionally, or the laundry done when he got off a long shift.

He let off the accelerator as they entered the town. A quick check of his mirrors showed him Cassie had done the same. The streets of Jasper were dark now. Only the occasional lamp glowed in windows as they passed. The businesses were all locked down for the night. Steering around the town square with its floodlit gazebo and trio of flagpoles, he tapped the brakes and hooked a right onto Main Street.

The parking lot adjacent to the Jasper Police Department held only a few cars. The cruisers driven by the officers on duty were gone, but they had a dispatcher working overnight. As usual, he spotted Dillon's truck parked in the space farthest from the door.

His friend was here even though they were both technically off duty, but in a town the size of Jasper, when a situation such as this arose, it was all-hands-on-deck. The other canine officer, Cal Hoover, was a family man, but Brady knew he'd join the search the second they called. He parked next to Dillon, then waited until Cassie pulled into a space as well.

He glanced over at his partner and found Winnie

dozing in her harness. Periods of intense searching zapped the usually energetic dog. Reaching across the seat, he stroked her smooth head and gave one of her silky ears a gentle tug. "A few minutes longer, girl. Let's go in and see what Dillon's got, then we'll go home and get a couple hours of sleep." He peered into the dog's drowsy amber eyes. "Sound like a plan?"

Winnie huffed a sigh, then nestled her face into his palm, demanding a few more strokes. He obliged her. After a final pat, he reached for the driver's door and climbed down from the truck. He attached the lead to Winnie's harness, then gave her room to jump down.

Cassie sat in her minivan, her hands wrapped tight around the steering wheel and her gaze locked on the brick wall of the police station. She was obviously deep in thought, and he hated to interrupt her, but every minute they spent gathering information brought them closer to finding her girls.

He wanted to hear what Dillon had unearthed on the ex-husband. And he wanted to get whatever information he could on this Keith Norton character Cassie seemed to think was more of a threat. In his experience, victims of harassment often had a heightened sixth sense when it came to their safety, and he'd worked enough domestic calls to take her concerns seriously.

Protocol said they had to cross one off before they could move on to the other, but regulations didn't mean he couldn't start gathering more intel.

Beside him, Winnie let out a soft whine. She was undoubtedly thirsty and ready for a rest. He could go ahead on into the station and get his dog situated, but something about Cassie Whitaker's rigid posture held him there.

She was barely holding it together. Who could blame her? He certainly didn't. But for his purposes, and for the sake of the investigation, he needed her to hang on a bit longer. Wincing to himself, he stepped over to the van and rapped on the window with the knuckle of his index finger.

Cassie jumped and he grimaced. When she looked over at him wide-eyed and wary, he gave her an apologetic wince and mouthed the word *Sorry.*

He noted her slumped shoulders and decided he needed to get her inside and get what information he could from her. When she opened her door, he automatically offered a hand to help her from the van, and to his surprise, she took it.

CASSIE HAD NEVER been inside the Jasper Police Department, but she'd been in others. When she left Billings, she vowed to herself she'd never visit another. Now, here she was. The low brick building sat squarely on Main Street just off the square. It had a solid kind of midcentury construction that somehow managed to look modern and old-fashioned all at once.

She forced herself to take three deep breaths after switching off the ignition.

Her girls were gone.

Her girls were her everything.

It felt like someone chopped both her arms off at once. What was she going to do if anything happened to them? How would she go on?

For the last few years, her entire world was a bubble built for three. In the months following her divorce from Mark, all she could do was focus on rebuilding. She wanted to give them the stable home they deserved, and maybe find a smidge of peace for herself.

Thankfully, Jilly didn't remember much about living with their dad, but Brook… Brook had seen too much. As a matter of fact, her older daughter had been the reason she finally said enough is enough and left.

It was one thing to live a life you didn't deserve; it was another to have your children witness it.

Mark, her ex-husband, had been an alcoholic, an ugly drunk who'd had no qualms about using his words to wound. Cassie had been about to leave him when she discovered she was pregnant with their second child. Feeling well and truly trapped, she stayed.

Until the night he went too far.

A tap on her window jolted her from her thoughts. She looked over to see Brady standing on the passenger side of her van, watching her with a cautious expression. She reached for the handle on her door.

She gathered her purse, opened her door, and hopped down from the vehicle. "Sorry, I was woolgathering."

Brady gave her a commiserating look when she came around the front of the car. "Understandable. It's been a lot to process." He swept an arm toward the building. "Let's go in and see what Diaz has found."

Diaz? It took a minute for Cassie to realize he was referring to the other officer at the scene. Dillon. He had introduced himself as Dillon Diaz. "You both have police dogs. Is Officer Diaz your partner or something?" she asked as they approached the front of the building.

One corner of Brady's mouth twitched. "Winnie is

my partner. The department here isn't really big enough to pair us off. For the most part, we all work together. I'll be the lead on this case, since it's a search and rescue, but Dillon and all the other officers will pitch in where they can."

"Oh. Yeah. Makes sense," she said as she passed through the door he held open for her.

She glanced down when Winnie brushed against her leg. The yellow Lab trotted beside her. Apparently, she decided Cassie needed backup more than Brady. She studied the dog Jilly had been so excited to greet mere hours earlier, then cast a shy glance at Brady. "Can I pet her? Is it okay?"

He nodded. "She's not on an active search at the moment, so I'm sure she would love a good rub behind the ears," he said with a wry grin. "Truthfully, she's kind of a needy girl, so she'll take whatever you give her."

Cassie reached down and stroked the dog's head, her fingertips grazing Winnie's silky years. "I've always heard you weren't supposed to pet service dogs on duty."

Brady shrugged. "True. But when she's focused, she's focused. You saw her out on the trail. She knows what her job is and she's good at it." He looked down at the Lab leaning heavily against Cassie's leg and gave a rueful chuckle. "And she's also keenly aware of when she's off duty."

"I'm glad." Cassie cringed as the words clogged in her throat. "I'm also glad she's off duty right now, because I sure could use some comfort."

Brady pointed to a chair beside the desk. "This is mine. Have a seat."

She took in the computer monitor covered in sticky notes and overflowing inbox as she lowered herself onto the hard wooden chair.

He shifted his attention to the dog, waited until she met his gaze, then pointed to Cassie. "Stay with her."

The Lab plopped down next to the chair, and placed her chin on Cassie's thigh. A surprised laugh of delight escaped her despite the crushing worry. "Oh wow."

"Good girl," he said to the dog. He shifted his attention to Cassie. "She takes cuddling seriously as well. Can I get you anything? Coffee? Water? Soda?"

She wanted to say "My kids," but she knew it wouldn't be fair. This man was trying to help as best he could. She had no cause to make him feel bad even though she felt wretched. She kept her answer short, hoping to avoid word vomiting her every thought all over the poor guy. "I'm good."

He hooked a thumb over his shoulder to the next desk, where Dillon Diaz sat speaking into a telephone. "I'm gonna grab us all a bottle of water. Hopefully, Dillon will be off the line by then and give us an update on where we are with your ex."

He glanced down at her hand on the dog's head. "Pet her as much as you want. It will never be too much for Winnie." He started to turn, then stopped. "Oh, and she really enjoys a nice solid hug if you need one."

The offer startled another laugh from her. "Oh, I need one."

Brady snapped his fingers twice. The dog lifted her chin and fixed her gaze on him. "Hug it out," he commanded.

Winnie gave an enthusiastic thump of her tail, then

rose on her hind legs. She placed her paws squarely on Cassie's lap, smiling as the two of them came face-to-face.

Cassie couldn't help but think of how delighted Jilly would have been to be on the receiving end of one of Winnie's hugs. Unable to contain it one second longer, she buried her face in the dog's soft neck, and the dam burst with a sob.

Chapter Six

Brady skirted his way over to Dillon's desk, hoping to put himself between the weeping woman and the other man. She'd had a hell of a night and deserved at least a few minutes of privacy.

"Any luck on the ex?" he asked. Dillon shook his head as he ended the call. "Phone's going straight to voice mail. I'm guessing it's either dead or he doesn't accept calls from unknown numbers. I left a message but with no real details."

Brady sat down in the chair alongside Dillon's desk. "The mother doesn't think it's the ex," he stated flatly. "Apparently, there was some guy she dated after the divorce who didn't take the breakup well. I don't have all the details, but I have a feeling he's been pursuing the relationship despite her moving to Jasper."

Dillon clicked his mouse and opened a fresh document. "You think we have a stalker situation going on?" he asked as he typed in the words, "Second possible suspect—Whitaker kidnapping" at the top of a page.

Seeing the word spelled out on the screen gave Brady a jolt. Kidnapping was a federal offense. Federal agents would probably be on the case midmorning. Something about the prospect of handing the case over made his stomach tighten. It wasn't simply a local department's desire to hang on to a case. He'd met these girls. He looked into those big, hopeful eyes. He watched them hug and shower love on Winnie. Turning his head, he saw Cassie Whitaker straightening in her chair, wiping her eyes with the heel of one hand while stroking Winnie's damp fur with the other. This case was personal. The last thing he wanted to do was hand it over to the Feds.

To Dillon, he said, "I'm going to get as much information on the ex-boyfriend as I can. Keith Norton is the name, and apparently they met after she moved from Billings to Bozeman, Montana."

Dillon typed the information into the notes document he'd started. "I'll run the usual searches and see if anything hits on the name. Keep me in the loop if you get anything more from the mom."

Brady rose and tapped two fingers on Dillon's desk. "Winnie and I will be heading out at first light—"

"Bentley and I will be there with you," Dillon said, glancing down at the dog sleeping beside his chair. "And three dogs are better than two. I'll call Hoover and make sure he brings Ruby too."

Brady clapped his friend on the shoulder. "Thanks, man." Crouching down to pat Dillon's dog, he said, "Rest, Bent. We're going to go at it hard first thing in the morning."

The dog's ears twitched and his tail thumped once, but it was all the acknowledgment he was given.

Snagging some bottles of water from the fridge, he

walked to his own desk and extended one wordlessly in Cassie's direction.

She accepted it, her cheeks coloring as she ducked her head. "Sorry about the, uh, meltdown."

Brady dropped into his own chair and looked directly at her. "Absolutely no need to apologize. It's the people who are too calm that worry me."

Cassie's brows shot skyward and she looked at him quizzically. "What do you mean?"

"Nothing," he answered a shade too quickly. He cracked the seal on one of the bottles and tipped the contents into the dog bowl beside his desk.

He wanted to kick himself. He was trying to build trust with her, and the last thing he needed to do was make her think he doubted her in any way. Still, it was a legitimate line of thinking. Some parents did stage the abduction of their child. But he knew in his gut they weren't dealing with such a case here.

There were a thousand different motives for kidnapping, but the outcomes in these situations were limited to a handful. The best was when the child was found safe and returned to a loving family. Good, but not great, were the cases when the child was found unharmed, then shuffled over to Child Protective Services. Worse was when the child was found, but not safe. But the worst of all were the cases when the child was never found.

"Nothing," he repeated more forcefully. "I'm running various scenarios through my head."

"And one of those scenarios concerns me arranging to have my own children taken?"

"You would not be the first, but no, we're sure you didn't," he stated firmly, holding her gaze.

She didn't flinch. If anything, her stubborn chin rose a notch. "Good, because someone took my babies and I want them home with me now," she said, enunciating each word for emphasis.

"Dillon has not been able to reach your ex-husband. We're going to pursue contacting him through the night, but as the children's father, he will be considered the number one suspect until we can eliminate him from the list."

Brady didn't bother to boot up his computer. Instead, he pulled a notepad out of one of the desk drawers and plucked a pen from a cup. Clicking it a couple times, he found her staring at him intently.

"But I want to get some information on this Keith Norton guy. Everything you can think of about him. If we're able to clear your ex, I want to have a bead on this guy, if I can."

"I met him at work. But I didn't start dating him then." She stopped, then gave her head a shake. "I took a temp job as a receptionist for a dental practice, and he was one of the dentists. I only worked there for a week, then landed a permanent job. A few months later I had the brilliant idea to try some online dating."

Color came into her cheeks, but she didn't avert her gaze. "I was still pretty new in town and hadn't met many people outside of work or my apartment building."

He bobbed his head. "I get you."

"Keith and I were a match, and since we'd already met each other, I thought it might be the safer thing to do," she said, wrinkling her nose at the thought. "Anyway, we dated for about six weeks. Dinner or the occasional movie. There was a high school girl who lived in the apartment next to mine who was willing to babysit. I thought I had a really good setup." She let out a sigh, then went silent.

Brady continued scribbling notes on his pad until he caught up with her. "Sounds reasonable enough," he said gently. "Go on."

"Keith only met the girls a couple of times when he came to the apartment to pick me up. I didn't like the thought of exposing them to anyone I was seeing until I thought the relationship might work, but logistically it seemed to make more sense for him to drive a couple of times. Or so he said," she spoke with a hard edge to her tone. "In hindsight, I think maybe he wanted to see where I lived. He made a point of wanting to meet the girls, so I introduced them, but they didn't spend hours together or anything. When you're a parent, you're always worried about who you're letting into your kids' lives, you know?"

Brady continued to write. "Absolutely."

"The last couple weeks we were seeing each other, life got hectic and I didn't have much energy left over for dating. He started to get pushy, and I made it clear the girls would always be my priority—"

Brady's head lifted. "Can you tell me what you mean by pushy?"

"Nothing physical," she said quickly. "More phone calls and texts. He even emailed a couple of times, trying to nail down when we might get together. I felt bad, but Brook had a cold, then gave it to the rest of us. The last thing on my mind was going out. I tried to explain to him, tried to tell him I'm the one who takes care of all three of us when we're sick, but he used it as an excuse to come over. He wanted to bring chicken soup, and I didn't have the energy. I told him I was too tired, and he didn't take it well."

"What did he do?"

"He came over unannounced with a bag of take-out chicken soup in his hand. I didn't want to open the door because I was sick, and the girls were sick, and the place was a mess." She shook her head, her lips tightening. "I looked like death warmed over on a plate, so I asked him to leave it at the door, and he started shouting about how he wasn't some kind of delivery service, and how it wasn't out of line for a guy to want to take care of his girlfriend."

She looked at him squarely.

"It bothered me he considered me his girlfriend. I wasn't in the right headspace for a relationship, and I didn't want to be. My marriage was a hot mess, and while I enjoyed having some adult companionship, I wasn't looking for anything serious. I even put it in my dating profile," she said, jabbing a finger at the notepad, insisting he make note of it as well.

"But he wanted to get serious," Brady filled in.

"I didn't think I was leading him on, but apparently Keith disagreed. Over the next few weeks, I changed my phone number and stopped replying to his emails after sending a polite one saying I didn't think things were going to work out."

"Then what happened?" Brady asked, because he'd taken enough of these statements to get the notion something had to have pushed her to flee Bozeman for Jasper.

"One day I got off work and went to get the girls from after-school care." She drew a shaky breath. "When I got there, I found Keith at the front desk arguing with the woman in charge. He was claiming he should have been on the list of people approved to check them out. The only people I had on my list were me and Kayla Mikelson's mother. She's the girl who lived next door and would sometimes babysit for me."

Brady focused intently on her. "What did he say when he saw you?"

"He tried to play it off like we'd arranged for him to get the girls, but I'd forgotten to put him on the list. I didn't want to make a scene, so I said something about how I was able to make it after all, thanked him and told him he could go. He was smart enough to get out of there."

She took a deep, shuddering breath. "I waited a while, looking at all their projects and artwork and stuff, hoping he'd be long gone when we came out. Thankfully, he was." She glanced down at the hand buried in the scruff of Winnie's neck. "I called Aunt Vera on my way home. She's the only family I have. My parents were killed in a car crash not long after I married Mark. She told me to pack my stuff and get to Jasper. My grandparents' house was vacant, and she said Millard would let me work at the diner until I found something permanent."

Leaning down, she pressed a kiss to the top of Winnie's head. Then, she whispered her secret into his dog's floppy ear, saying, "We left Bozeman as soon as I could pack my car, but somehow, he always keeps tabs on me."

"How do you mean?"

"I changed phone numbers, but he managed to get the new one and started calling and texting again." She sighed and slumped down in the chair, like merely talking about the man sapped her energy. "I've changed my number twice now. I also closed all my social media accounts, thinking maybe he was tracking me through a mutual friend or something."

She paused until he met her gaze. With a meaningful glance over at Dillon, she pitched her voice low.

"Here's the thing. I get why you have to look at Mark first, but I can tell you he doesn't care what happens to me or the girls. He's a drunk. A mean drunk, and not a good guy to be married to, but his first thought is always about his next drink."

Brady flinched when she reached across and tapped the pad where he'd been scrawling notes. He looked down at everything he'd written. His handwriting was a barely legible mix of print and cursive. He'd be hard-pressed to make out some of the words in the morning. Then she spoke with a soft surety that startled him from any worries over his penmanship.

"Keith," she whispered. "If anyone from my past did this, he would be the one."

Chapter Seven

Given what she'd shared with him about the former boyfriend, Brady was inclined to agree with Cassie's assessment. Still, they couldn't search until morning, and
his captain wasn't going to let him go off on too many
tangents until Mark Whitaker was located.

But her story, combined with the steady determination in her hazel eyes, sold him on the notion of Keith
Norton as the guy. The person who'd lured the girls
from the party was someone they knew. According to
the volunteers they'd spoken to, and the boy who'd seen
them leave, they hadn't fussed about exiting the games
area with him.

He drummed the pen against the pad. The temptation
to try to lure this Norton guy out was strong. But if he
did have the girls, if he was fixated on Cassie, would
it put them in more danger if he knew she suspected
him? If she'd changed phone numbers, would she still
be able to reach the man?

"Do you still have his phone number?" Brady
winced. He'd meant to be gentler with the request, but
he was tired, and this might be something.

But Cassie didn't hesitate. She pulled her phone from

her pocket and unlocked it. "I've kept it. I also have screenshots, archived emails and all of it," she said as she swiped at the screen.

He must have made a sound of surprise because she lifted an eyebrow.

"In less than a decade, I've managed to get involved with two of the most despicable men I've ever met. I've learned a few lessons, Officer Nichols."

As she said the last, she thrust the phone at him. The contact page labeled Dr. Keith Norton had a lock icon at the top. Nearly every field was completed. Name, address, email, various phone numbers. It appeared she had collected as much data on the man as she could find.

"It's Brady," he corrected. "And do you mind if I send this to my phone?"

"Please do."

He transferred the information to his own number, then saved his contact information to her phone. "I saved my contact info for you, in case you need me," he informed her.

"Thank you."

He eyed the information she'd gathered on her former paramour, weighing whether he should ask her to put herself out there. Bracing himself to be shut down, he went for it. "Are you willing to try to reach out to this guy?"

She squirmed when he handed her phone to her. "You want me to call him?"

He could see she was uncomfortable with the idea. "I'm thinking maybe. We could try to pinpoint his location."

"He's smart about technology. I doubt he's carrying

his phone," she said, frowning at the number on her screen. "He tags every photo he takes. He knows his phone has GPS."

"Maybe not, but it could be worth a try to see if we can determine whether he's even in the area."

She gnawed on her bottom lip, then gave a decisive nod. "Okay. How do we do this? I don't want to call him from this phone. I don't want him to have this number."

Brady pushed away from the desk. "No problem. Give me a minute."

He walked over to Dillon's desk and waited until his friend looked up from his screen.

"Hey, do we still have any of those burner phones we used to trace calls when we were tracking those dealers?" he asked, referencing a methamphetamine bust they'd helped assist with a few months prior.

Dillon glanced at a metal cabinet in the corner of the room. "Yeah, there are a couple in there. We'll probably have to update the software to make sure we can run a trace on them. Then we can triangulate any signal we get."

Brady started in that direction. "I'm going to get one. Would you check the software? We want to try to ping this ex-boyfriend's phone and see if we can get coordinates in the vicinity."

Dillon shot to his feet. "Good idea. We'll have her try the ex-husband's phone too. It's better than nothing."

"I agree." Brady walked to the cabinet, then called over his shoulder. "Cassie? Do you have a phone number for your ex as well?"

He pulled a pay-as-you-go phone still in its package from the supply cabinet and tossed it to Dillon. His friend caught it and went to work plugging the phone's information into the software on his computer. When they made it to his desk, he saw Cassie had a contact labeled simply Mark showing on her phone.

"This is the latest number I have, but I have no idea if he's still using it. He tends to forget to pay his phone bill. After a while, the cellular companies cut him off and he has to move on to a different one."

"We're going to try something with some software we have. It may not amount to much, but it's something," he said with a shrug.

Cassie handed over her phone again. "I'll do anything. I don't have any idea how I'm going to make it till morning."

At her feet, Winnie let out a small snuffle as if she'd heard and agreed wholeheartedly, even though the dog was clearly half asleep.

Brady felt the exact same way. "It's always better to feel like you're doing something rather than nothing. Let's try this, then we're all going to head home and get some rest. Dillon and Bentley will be heading out to search with us first thing in the morning."

Dillon approached holding the newly programmed phone, and she eyed it warily. "What do you need me to do?" she asked, wringing her hands again.

"You don't need to say anything," Brady assured her. "We're going to dial the number and on the off chance he answers, mute it. But it will be an unknown number, so even if he lets it go to voice mail, hang on. We're hoping the software will get a ping on the phone receiving the call. From there, we may be able to determine where it's located. You don't have to speak at all," he said. "As a matter of fact, it's better if you don't."

"Okay," she agreed. "I'm not so worried about Mark, but what if Keith has something on his phone capable of finding this one?" she asked, nodding to the burner phone.

Dillon shook his head. "The software we use scrambles everything. If he tries to pin it down, all it will show is a data farm in Silicon Valley."

The three of them leaned over the desk as Brady punched in the numbers for Mark Whitaker's mobile phone. It rang and rang until finally voice mail connected, and a gruff-sounding man said only, "Leave a message. Maybe I'll call you."

The three of them stood in silence, letting the recording spool out on the voice mail until the service tripped over to an automated recording asking them if they were satisfied with the recording. Brady glanced over at Dillon, and the other man gave a silent nod. He disconnected the call, then waited until the screen went dark again. He looked over at his friend.

"You got a location?"

"Yep," Dillon said. "Looks to be someplace in the middle of Billings, Montana. I'll get the coordinates and pinpoint a more exact address. In the meantime, let's try the numbers for the other guy," he suggested.

Brady chanced a glance at Cassie and found her twisting her fingers together in her lap. "Okay so far?" he asked.

"As okay as I'm going to be," she said grimly. "Let's do it."

"Ready?" he called to Dillon.

"Go for it," the other man replied.

Brady dialed the first number Cassie had listed on Norton's contact page. As expected, the call went to voice mail. They held their breath, allowing the recording to take in the silence for as long as it would allow, then Brady disconnected when Dillon knocked on his desktop.

"Bozeman, Montana," he announced a minute later.

Cassie let out an explosion of breath. "Oh God. I don't know if I was wanting him to answer and be here, or if I wanted it not to be him." Her head swiveled and she stared at him, her eyes wide with panic. "Which would be worse? Somebody we know or a stranger? But they wouldn't go off with a stranger. I've taught them better," she insisted.

"I'm sure you have," Brady said calmly. "But let's not assume anything until we try these other numbers you have here. If he's as smart as you say he is, he may have left this most recent phone at home. Or it's not his only phone."

Cassie lifted a trembling hand to her mouth, but nodded her assent. Brady glanced at Dillon and asked, "Ready to run another?"

"Ready when you are," his friend replied.

Brady punched in the second phone number and got a recording saying it was no longer in service. He let it play out in hopes something might register on the software, but Dillon only gave a short shake of his head.

"Okay, on to the next," he murmured under his breath.

Brady dialed the third and final phone number, and they all waited as it rang and rang. At last, the voice mail kicked in and they let the recording run on as long as they could.

Behind him, Dillon rapped sharply on the desk three times. Brady disconnected the call and whirled. "You get something?" he demanded.

Dillon scribbled a couple of things on a notepad, then began typing furiously on his computer keyboard. "White Feather, Idaho. Getting the GPS coordinates. I'll get the address and see if I can send the sheriff out to the location."

Cassie slowly lowered her hand. "Oh, my God. It *is* him," she said, her voice throaty with disbelief.

When she looked at Brady, her expression was a mixture of hope and fear so potent, he felt both viscerally.

"I don't think he'd hurt them," she said in a whisper. "He's not a violent man. At least I don't think he is. Mark could get out of control, so I was attuned to the signs, and I never saw anything violent in Keith," she said, almost to reassure him more than herself.

But Brady was fixated on what she said about her ex-husband. "What do you mean Mark could get out of control?"

Cassie closed her eyes, drew in a deep breath, then exhaled slowly. "He pushed me around... Never punched me or anything, but there were a couple of times he shoved me into things—furniture, doors, whatever. He drank too much. One night we were having a fight and Brook came out of her room. We'd woken her. He pushed her aside...hard..." She stopped on a tangled sob.

"Take your time," he said in his most soothing tone. He nudged the bottle of water closer to her, and Cassie reached out and grabbed it like a lifeline. Brady watched as she unscrewed the cap with trembling hands, took a small sip and then carefully replaced the cap.

"He shoved her into a wall and I lost my mind. I went at him, kicking and screaming and throwing punches until he finally fell. Then I pulled my daddy's old hunting rifle from the closet and told him I'd load it and unload into him if he ever touched one of my children again."

"Take a sip," he urged, his tone low and soothing.

She did as he suggested, then blew out a breath. "I packed the girls, the gun, and left. I can still hear him standing in the driveway yelling about how I'd be crawling to him by the next morning. I'd never be able to make it without him…blah, blah, blah." She wet her lips, then met Brady's gaze steadily. "I did. We never went home again. No one hurts my girls."

"I have no doubt."

Chapter Eight

He said it with such quiet certainty, Cassie found she had no room for disbelief. Which was good. She spent far too long doubting herself and her ability to be a good mother to her girls. And though some could argue her current predicament might indicate she wasn't exactly mother of the year, Cassie refused to accept the blame for somebody else's actions. Being married to an abusive alcoholic had taught her a thing or two about personal responsibility. She was not going to blame herself for this situation.

"What do we do now?" she asked, sounding considerably steadier than she felt on the inside.

"Dillon's going to call the sheriff's department and have them do a drive-by to see if they can get anyone who has seen Keith in the area. I'm gonna need you to give me as good a physical description as you possibly can."

Cassie barked a laugh. "I can do better."

Snatching her phone again, she scrolled through her photos until she came across the one Keith had insisted they take together. They'd had dinner at a popular local restaurant, and then had gone for a walk after sharing a dessert. She'd been startled when he stopped another couple on the sidewalk and asked the woman to snap their picture, but she hadn't objected. The gesture had seemed impulsive and romantic. Until the woman had handed his phone to him and Keith had expertly enhanced and cropped the photo with a few taps of the screen. He'd texted it to her and urged her to save it to her camera roll. She did, then promptly forgotten about it until now.

Brook and Jilly had had a dance recital the following weekend, and the photo of her and Keith was soon swallowed by dozens of shots of her daughters dressed in cowgirl costumes and sparkling with glitter.

Brady eyeballed the photo. "This is helpful." He tapped the phone screen and quickly sent the photo to his own phone. Then he clicked his pen once more. "I'm guessing from the photo about five-eleven or six feet?" he asked, all business once again.

"I'm five-seven, so I'm going to say somewhere closer to five-ten or five-eleven. I don't think he was over six feet tall."

Brady scribbled it down. "Build?"

Cassie winced. She and Keith had been intimate exactly twice, but given the current context, it was hard to imagine she was describing the same man. He'd seemed so…normal. Forcing herself to focus on recounting facts as she knew them, she drew a deep breath and said, "Lean, somewhat muscular, but not bulky. He was a runner. Kept talking about training for a triathlon, but I don't think he's ever gotten far. It was all talk. A lot of things with Keith were all talk."

"A shade under six foot, lean build but not skinny," Brady repeated. "Any distinguishing marks, tattoos, scars, anything notable?"

She shook her head. "No. He was a pretty average-looking guy. Handsome enough. Looked like a guy out of sitcom central casting for nice-guy-slash-dentist-or-doctor. Brown hair, brownish eyes, not too fair, not too tan. Everything about him was sort of medium," she concluded.

"What about how he dressed? Anything unusual there? Did he wear a hat? Was he a ball cap guy or one of those who fancied himself a cowboy?"

She shook her head. "No hats. Didn't like to have his hair messed."

"Got it." Brady clicked his pen, then tapped the tablet. Turning to look her directly in the eye, he said "You've done well here. You've given us far more information than most people can. We have a lot to go on."

She knew his words were meant to comfort her. It was a compliment. A pat on the head meant to reassure her, but his kindness only made her previous choices seem worse. What kind of woman needed to keep a dossier on a man she dated for barely two months?

The kind who'd been through the wringer with another man.

"I got an address and sent it on to the sheriff's department," Dillon called out from behind him. He rose from his desk, and Bentley rose as well. "We're going to head home, but as soon as I get any word from the sheriff, I'll relay it to Brady and he can pass it along to you." He and Bentley walked over to Brady's desk, where the two dogs exchanged a sniff.

Brady extended a hand to his friend. "Appreciate your help, man."

Dillon raised a hand. "Anytime." He checked his watch. "See you at about five thirty?" he asked.

"I'll be by about five fifteen," Brady informed him. "It should be getting light by five forty-five. I want to be at the road when it does."

Dillon extended his hand to Cassie. Shocked, she took it and gave it a firm shake, but to her surprise, Dillon covered hers with his other hand, enveloping her in a warm grip.

"I'm not going to tell you not to worry because I don't believe in asking for the impossible. I *am* going to tell you we will not stop—" he tipped his head toward Brady and then looked down at the dogs at their feet "—until we find your girls. And we will."

Cassie drew her hand away slowly, and curled it into a fist over her heart. "Thank you."

Dillon stepped away. "Call you as soon as I hear anything on the ex," he said in parting.

The door closed behind him, and Cassie became hyperaware she was alone with Brady Nichols. She fidgeted in her seat, and Winnie scrambled onto her front paws, her expression concerned as she leaned into Cassie once more. "Wow, she *is* intuitive, isn't she?" she said with a laugh.

"When Emma was training her, it was a tough call to decide whether she'd be better off doing search and rescue or counseling and emotional support."

"She seems to be a pro at both."

Brady chuckled. "Winnie is a dog of many talents. Not only is she a search and rescue expert, and a part-time empath, but she also excels in devouring enormous dog bones and has occasionally gnawed on large pieces of furniture."

"Large pieces of furniture?" she asked, brows raised.

He shrugged. "I never liked the couch anyway."

Cassie laughed out loud, and the sound startled her so much she had to cover her mouth with her hand. Winnie lifted a paw in silent plea for some attention. Shaking her head, Cassie leaned forward and used both hands to stroke the fur over the dog's head and down her neck. "Am I comforting her or is she comforting me?" she asked him in a low, amused tone.

"Whatever works," Brady told her.

"She's wonderful," she murmured as she hugged the dog again.

"You'd be questioning your assessment if she ate your couch," he said dryly. "We should all get home. We have a busy morning coming."

"Aren't we gonna wait until we hear from the sheriff?"

"My number is in your phone. I will text you as soon as I get any news, but we all have to get what rest we can. Tomorrow's going to be a busy day."

Cassie stood, but she didn't reach for her bag. "I don't want to go home without them." It was the truth, though she was embarrassed to have blurted it out. She could not imagine walking into her house without Brook and Jilly by her side.

"Is there anywhere else you can stay tonight?"

"Aunt Vera said I could stay there," she said, gathering her bag, relieved to have decided at last.

She pulled her keys from the depths of her purse. When she met his gaze again, she felt something settle deep inside her. She wanted to say more, but she wasn't sure what. Jingling her keys in her palm, she glanced at him, needing one last dose of reassurance. "You'll call?"

He inclined his head. "The second I hear anything."

"Thank you. Good night."

She stepped outside and a brisk breeze cut through her thin summer clothes. She ducked her head and climbed into her van, her limbs feeling like they were filled with wet cement. Cool moisture streaked from her eyes. Dashing the tears away, she tossed her bag onto the passenger seat and tried to ignore the sickly sweet scent of juice spilled onto the carpet. She started the engine, but her phone chimed.

She thrust her hand into the outer pocket of the bag and fumbled until she could get the text to open.

Sheriff's dept rpts no one home at addr, no vehicle. ?ing neighbors with the help of your pic. Try to sleep.

Try to sleep. The last part made her want to snort, but it caught on a sob. Brady Nichols could walk out of the building any second now, so she typed only a brief reply in thanks, then threw the van into Reverse and swung out of the spot. He'd seen her cry enough for one night. As she pulled out of the parking lot, she vowed she'd hold herself together better tomorrow. Poor Winnie had a job to do, and she wouldn't be able to help find her girls if she had a distraught mother crying into her soft fur.

After hooking a right and pointing the van toward her aunt and uncle's house, Cassie decided to rethink her stance on getting a dog for the girls.

Chapter Nine

Cassie parked in front of her aunt and uncle's house and entered through the kitchen door, which, as usual, they'd left unlocked. Frowning, she twisted the dead bolt. It was stiff from disuse and didn't align correctly, but she threw a hip against the door and the bolt slid home.

The house was cloaked in darkness, save for the light above the stove. She'd closed the door as quietly as she could, hoping she wouldn't disturb her aunt and uncle's sleep. They rose at four thirty each morning to start preparing the diner for the breakfast rush, and the last thing she wanted to do was cut into their rest.

Leaving the light on, she tiptoed through the kitchen to the hall, but a voice from the darkened living room stopped her in her tracks.

"I take it there's no news?"

Cassie jumped and whirled, pressing her hand flat to her chest to hold her thumping heart inside her rib cage. She squinted into the darkness and saw Aunt Vera seated on the worn sofa, her hands wrapped around a mug. "Oh, my goodness, you scared me," she said in a rush.

"Sorry, baby girl."

The endearment, the same one the usually no-nonsense Vera used for her great-nieces, made a lump the size of her fist lodge at the base of Cassie's throat.

She swallowed hard. "I'm sorry. I thought you'd be in bed, and I was trying to be quiet."

"Who can sleep?" Vera replied gruffly.

Cassie stepped into the darkened room. "Hopefully Millard?" Cassie said tiredly. Her uncle was a good man, a kind man, but he guarded his sleep jealously and was notoriously cranky if he didn't get at least seven hours in the sack.

The corners of Vera's mouth twitched as she patted the cushion beside her in invitation. "He's in there sawing logs."

"Good." Cassie lowered herself to the sofa beside her aunt, and to her surprise, Vera stretched an arm around her, gently urging Cassie to lean into her. Too tired to resist getting what comfort was offered, she toppled over until her head rested on Vera's lap.

"No, there's no news," she whispered, nearly choking on the words. "They're trying to locate Mark but not having any luck."

Vera snorted. "Mark. He'd never stir himself enough to help himself to his children," she said disdainfully. She reached over and placed the mug on the end table. "I'll tell you who I'm worried about—it's that Keith fella," her aunt insisted. "I told the chief he was the one they need to be looking for when we were at Emma's place, but I don't think he was paying me any mind."

Cassie sniffled but had to stifle a laugh at the thought of her opinionated and outspoken aunt being ignored.

Vera didn't mince words, but most of the residents of Jasper were used to her bluntness.

"I agree. I told Officer Nichols all about Keith, and I'm pretty sure they're going to focus in on him too, but they have to make sure Mark is in the clear first since he's their father."

Vera shook her head, her expression mournful. "It's a sad, sorry day when folks can't let their kids run around here in Jasper. You expect to hear about things like this happening in the big city. Heck, I thought even Boise was fairly safe, but now…"

"It happens everywhere," Cassie said, hoarse with fatigue and emotion.

The two women fell silent. Vera ran a hand over Cassie's hair. The gesture was another surprise in an evening chock-full of them. Vera was awkward and self-conscious with her affections, which, to Cassie's mind, made them even more endearing.

"You want a cup of tea? Something to help you sleep?" her aunt offered.

Cassie drew in a steadying breath. "No, thank you. Tea will only make me jittery." She forced herself to sit on her own, freeing her aunt of her weight. "You should try to get some sleep. I think I'm going to lie down and wait for the dawn."

Vera hoisted herself from her seat with a groan. "There are clean sheets on the spare bed. At least try to close your eyes. You'll want them well rested so you can help look for your girls," she said with a nod. "Folks will be out early. Millard and I will keep everybody fueled from the diner. Aside from the official search, a few of the guides from the outfitters are going to lead small groups on the hiking trails."

Cassie swallowed past the tightness in her chest. "I appreciate everyone's help."

"It's what folks around here do. We look out for each other," Vera said briskly. "You're one of ours, whether you've been living here your whole life or not. We're going to find your girls, and we're going to bring them home."

Vera placed a hard peck of a kiss to the top of Cassie's head, then shuffled toward the hall. "Now, get to bed," she ordered.

Cassie's heart thudded as she listened to her aunt's shuffling steps. She sat on the sofa for a few minutes more, simply staring into the middle distance and allowing the quiet of the house to close in around her. Thank goodness she didn't have to go home. Her grandparents' house, the house she shared with her girls, would be an entirely different sort of quiet, and it wasn't one Cassie thought she could handle.

Heeding her aunt's advice, she forced herself to rise and head down the hall as well. True to form, the guest room was neat as a pin. The wedding-ring-patterned quilt had been folded down, and faded floral sheets awaited her. Cassie stripped off the clothes she'd been wearing all day and slid between them in nothing more than her underwear. The pillowcase smelled like fabric softener and sunshine. Clutching the spare pillow to her chest, she rolled onto her side and allowed silent, shuddering tears to flow.

She must have cried herself to sleep because the next

thing she knew, gray light filled the room and someone was knocking on the front door.

Startled, she sprang from the bed. She didn't bother to dress. Her heart hammering, she yanked the quilt free and wrapped it around her. Holding the bundle of covers closed at her throat, she hurried toward the door. Out of habit, she checked through the sidelight first. Brady Nichols stood on the top step wearing dark tactical gear, sturdy black boots and a vest identifying him as a member of the Jasper PD. No jeans or T-shirt in sight. She fumbled to open the single lock charged with holding the big, bad world at bay.

She yanked open the door. "Have you heard anything?" she demanded in a rush of breath.

Brady's eyes widened when he took in her state of undress. But to his credit, he fixed his gaze directly on her forehead as he shook his head.

"Nothing about the girls. I was coming to tell you your ex-husband has been located. He spent the night as a guest of the Billings Police Department. We got the confirmation this morning. They've been holding him for drunk and disorderly conduct."

"No shock there," Cassie muttered.

"Norton has been bumped to number one on our list, but we need you to try to think if there's anyone else we should be looking at."

She shook her head. "No, there's no one else. And he's here in Idaho. What more do you need to convince you?"

"It's not a matter of convincing anyone. I want to be sure we're covering all the bases. I spoke to Dillon and they've found a vehicle they believe may be Norton's truck. They're running the plates now."

"His truck? Keith drives a car. A sedan," she said, her brow furrowing in confusion.

"There's a truck with a Montana temporary tag parked near the old ranger station. We're heading out there now."

Cassie blinked. "What do you mean heading out now? Without me?" She stared at him in bafflement. It never occurred to her the search would go on without her being there.

"It's better if you stay here. We can move faster without civilians on-site," he said, meeting her eyes.

"I'm not a civilian. I'm their mother."

"I'm aware, but—"

"No. No, you're not going out there without me." Leaving the front door wide-open, she backed into the house and took off at a run. In her haste, she let the quilt drop as she headed down the hallway, uncaring whether she'd flashed Officer Nichols or not. In the spare room, she yanked on her clothing. "Don't you dare leave without me," she shouted, then grimaced.

A glance at the clock by the bed told her Millard and Vera were likely already gone. She said a quick prayer of thanks for small favors and pulled her shirt over her head. Shoes dangling from her fingers, she finger-combed the snarls from her hair with her free hand as she headed for the front door. "I am their mama. I'm the one who they're gonna want to see the minute you find them."

Brady had stepped inside and allowed the screen

door to close behind him. "No doubt. But I thought I would call you once we found any sign—"

Cassie charged straight at him. She'd go through him if she had to. She was getting in his car. "No, sir. I'm going."

He deftly sidestepped her in the nick of time. "Listen, I understand—"

"Pull the door closed behind you," she called over her shoulder. "Millard and Vera will have already left for the diner, and I can't leave their house standing wide-open."

"Ms. Whitaker, I can't—"

"I think we're on a first-name basis now, don't you?" She headed for the passenger side of the officially marked K-9 unit he was driving and reached for the door handle. "Is Winnie in back?" she called out to him.

Brady pulled the front door closed and hurried down the concrete steps, the screen door slamming hard as he came after her. "Yes, but you can't climb in and ride along. This is an official investigation."

"And I'm officially their mama, and I'm not letting this go on without me being there. Period. Now, we can stand here and argue until the sun rises and sets again, but the clock is ticking." She opened the door, tossed her shoes inside, then jumped in after them, slamming the door on Brady's protests.

Chapter Ten

This had disaster written all over it. Brady drove toward the fire lane where they'd lost the trail the previous night with his jaw set. Dillon had called to say he was already on his way with Bentley. Cal Hoover and his dog, Ruby, were coming too. The chief had texted a heads-up that the FBI field office in Boise had been notified of the abduction. The ticking clock in his head grew louder. If he and Winnie wanted to be in on the search and rescue, he didn't have daylight to waste arguing with the mother of the victims.

But boy, was he gonna hear it from the guys.

"You didn't want to bring me, but I can't sit there and wait," she said, breaking the taut silence.

"It's not a matter of what I want," Brady explained. "There are procedures I have to follow." He drummed his fingers on the steering wheel, already anticipating the ribbing coming his way. But then, maybe he could mitigate some of it by keeping her out of sight. "When we get there, you have to stay in the vehicle. Our dogs are trained, but we want to give them as few mixed signals as we possibly can. Having you out there will add another scent to the mix."

"I'm not going to do anything to jeopardize your search for my daughters," she said stiffly. "But if you think I'm going to sit home waiting for you to call, you've lost your mind."

"Yes, you've made your stance abundantly clear," Brady answered in the same tone. "My primary concern is to keep the search area pristine. We have a new possible point of entry. If you go running willy-nilly into our search, it's only going to complicate matters."

"I've never run willy-nilly in my entire life," she replied tartly.

"Okay." He glanced at her again. "As long as you understand there are reasons I can't let you go traipsing off into the hills. There's a methodology to doing what we do. I want to be clear."

"Crystal clear," she said.

Brady pulled off the main highway onto the dirt lane leading into the foothills. He turned onto the fire lane, but ascended about a mile farther into the woods. The road widened slightly when the old ranger station came into view. He lifted his foot from the accelerator and allowed the tires to roll to a grumbling halt behind a pickup truck parked in the center of the lane.

"Montana temporary tag," she whispered.

Anxious to keep her focused until their backup arrived, he parked the SUV at an angle, effectively blocking the pickup in. "Have you ever seen this truck?"

She shook her head hard. "No. Never."

"Keith Norton does not own a truck?"

"Not that I'm aware of, but this one is obviously used," she said, gesturing to the vehicle. "Keith is a dentist. He makes a good living. He could easily afford to buy a used truck."

"Probably in cash," Brady murmured. "Tell me more about him. You said he's a runner. Does he hunt? Camp?"

She wagged her head hard. "No. God no. The opposite." The corner of her mouth lifted in a disdainful smirk. "He's a city guy. Not at all outdoorsy. I wanted to go for a hike when we were first seeing each other. I picked a supereasy trail, thinking it would be nice to walk and talk. All he did was complain."

"Complain about what?"

"The heat, the bugs, the dirt—" she waved a dismissive hand "—all of it." She paused when she caught sight of the rugged terrain beyond the small cabin. "He isn't the kind of guy who likes to get mussed."

"So sleeping out of doors—"

"I can't imagine he would."

"He never returned to the house in White Feather. The county sheriff had an eye on it all night."

"Maybe they slept in the truck?" she hazarded. "I should go look, see if there's any trace of the girls—" Cassie reached for her door handle, and he placed a staying hand on her arm. "No, ma'am. You stay in the vehicle, remember? Those are my conditions," he said, holding her belligerent gaze.

"Brady—"

"No. We wait for backup before we approach the vehicle, then you wait in here. If you can't agree to my terms, I will turn around, drive you to town and dump you there."

They glared at one another.

"Cassie, I need you to work with me here. Stay in the car. I promise you as soon as there's anything to tell, you will be told."

Their intense stare-down lasted a few more seconds. The sound of vehicles approaching snared her attention. She watched wide-eyed as three other vehicles—marked and unmarked—maneuvered around them to block the truck in from every possible angle. Finally, she acquiesced with a nod.

"You better have my contact information open on your phone and saved to your favorites," she warned. "We're talking speed dial ready. You get me?"

He reached for his own door handle, not allowing himself to dwell too long on the way she said his name. "Trust us. I promise you Winnie and I want to find them every bit as much as you do."

He closed the driver's door and moved to the lift gate of the SUV. He saw her turn in her seat, her eyes glued to him as he unhooked Winnie's restraint.

"Tell her we're gonna find her girls," he ordered the dog.

Winnie let out a low woof, and Brady was pretty sure he heard a soft sob escape Cassie when he slammed the lift gate closed.

THEY WERE TWO HOURS in and at least a mile from the cabin when the hairs on Brady's neck prickled. He stilled, and Winnie paused too. She lifted her nose from the mulchy ground and sniffed the air, her ears flicking forward as she caught something of interest on the wind.

"I feel it too," he said, speaking softly to his partner. "I think they were near here, don't you, girl?"

Winnie sniffed some more, her snout raised high and her forehead wrinkled in concentration. Brady didn't interfere. He didn't rush her or do anything more than stand by her side. He had all the faith in the world in this dog. Suddenly, Winnie jerked to the right and took off into the underbrush, straining at her lead. With a practiced flick of his thumb, Brady untethered the dog, allowing her to follow her nose at her own pace.

Fighting his way through the ever-thickening underbrush, he kept his attention fixed directly ahead of him. Barely three minutes passed when a sharp bark cut through the sound of his own labored breathing.

The radio affixed to his collar crackled, and Chief Walters asked, "Was that Winnie?"

Brady keyed the microphone. "Ten-four. She's onto something."

A burst of static came across, then Dillon's call came through. "Ping your current location so we can tighten the scope."

Brady did as his friend suggested, relaying his approximate position to the satellites orbiting the earth while he moved steadily in the direction of his dog's increasingly agitated barks.

"You get me?" he asked into the mic.

A second later, his fellow lieutenant, Cal Hoover, replied, "I have you."

"Ten-four," Dillon chimed in.

Brady checked his compass. "Winnie is heading almost due west. There's a bluff ahead, so I'm not sure what she—" He paused when he burst through a clump of undergrowth and saw his dog barking at the jagged rocks. About seven feet above the clearing, there looked to be a small crevice in the rock formation. Winnie's gaze was fixed on it with level-five Labrador intensity.

"There's a cave," he spoke the words quietly into his mic.

"Await backup," the chief ordered.

If asked, Brady would say he couldn't hear the man over the ruckus his dog was making. But if they found the Whitaker girls, the chief wouldn't ask too many questions. He was good about looking the other way when it was expedient.

Lowering his hand, he snapped his fingers once. Winnie toned her barking down to a stream of steady woofs. If there was anyone there, her barking would have already sent them deeper into the crevice or flushed them out, but he didn't want her to stop entirely. His team would use her barks as a beacon.

Climbing over the smaller boulders at the base of the rock face, he groped for a handhold. Five minutes and a few curses later, he leveraged himself high enough to peek over the ledge into the cave. There, he saw a small white sock, a pink elastic hair band and nothing more than a few footprints in the dust covering the rock.

"Crap."

He braced an elbow on the ledge and made a grab for the bits one of the girls had left behind. Jilly, he guessed, judging by the size of the sock and a heart-squeezing flash of memory. She'd had her long blond hair in two of these ponytail holders. And, presumably, she'd had two socks on as well, but he couldn't swear under oath.

Something wasn't adding up for him. For the life of him, Brady could not figure out exactly what the end game was. If he were going to kidnap a couple of kids, he would have hightailed it to the highway, not driven deeper into the wilderness. His gut told him Brook and Jilly were not who Norton—if it was indeed Cassie's former boyfriend—was after. Did he still have them, or had the jerk dumped the girls out here? What if he was camped out at Cassie's house while they were here searching?

A surge of hot panic shot through him as he climbed down onto the jagged rocks. Breathless, he pressed the button on his mic. "Does someone have eyes on Cassie Whitaker?"

A second later, Chief Walters's laconic drawl came through loud and clear. "You mean the civilian you have riding shotgun in your official vehicle, Lieutenant Nichols? Yes, I do."

Brady didn't have the inclination to be embarrassed by the subtle dressing-down. "Yes, sir. Keep tabs on her, will you? I don't think the kids are the end game here."

"What have you found, Nichols?" the chief asked, as Cal Hoover burst out of the woods, his dog, Ruby, at his side.

Brady held the sock and the hair tie, glanced at the cave one last time, then gave his head a shake to indicate the place was empty. Pulling the microphone from his shoulder, he spoke directly into it. "Sir, I have evidence they were in a cave on the northeast side of the outcropping, but nothing more at this time."

"I have an ETA of thirteen hundred from the federal agents," the chief informed him gruffly.

"Ten-four. We'll keep going until relieved," Brady replied. Or until they found the girls.

"I have an eye on things here," Chief Walters assured him.

"From the footprints I could see, it appears they are on the move," he reported.

"Then you get moving too. I'd like to put the lady's mind at ease. Once the Feds get here, she'll have to start this whole process over again."

"Ten-four. Me too, sir."

He crouched in front of Winnie and stared into the Lab's amber eyes until he was sure he held her full attention. Then he offered the sock for her to sniff. "Here, girl. Find," he commanded.

Winnie put her head down and paced the area in a slow, methodical circle. Brady watched her carefully, then offered a sniff of his findings to Cal's dog, Ruby. The German shepherd hadn't had time to take a good snort, when Winnie whipped her head to the right, barked twice and bounded into the woods again.

But this time, she was heading away from the mountain.

Chapter Eleven

Cassie appreciated the steadying presence of Chief Walters, but… She shot him a sidelong glance. "There's something they aren't telling me, isn't there?"

"There are likely a lot of things we aren't telling you, ma'am," the chief replied. He smoothed the rough edges of the comment away with a kindly pat on the arm. "Those are my best people. If they can't find them, the Feds are coming right behind with *their* best people. We're doing everything we can possibly do to get those girls home safe."

"I don't doubt it, Chief," Cassie said in a rush. "I feel so… I'm a mom," she said, holding her hands out in helpless futility. "I'm the one who does things. I'm not the one who waits."

He gave a brief nod. "They're on the right track. Believe me."

Chief Walters was right: she had to trust Brady would come through for her. Brady was the man who'd listened to her chronicle her pathetic excuse of a love life without batting a judgmental eyelash. Brady offered her reassurances and had spoken so gently and patiently with her girls. Until they moved to Jasper, Jilly and Brook hadn't had many good interactions with men outside of a school setting. They were just warming to her uncle, and Millard was one of the mildest men she'd ever met. Biting her lip, she paced the length of the SUV. Brady had been the first man she'd ever seen them approach without trepidation. But, of course, Winnie had been the real draw there.

She'd once been close to her father and enjoyed her uncle's company, but after what she'd been through with Mark, it was difficult not to be guarded. Perhaps she hadn't given Keith the chance he thought he deserved, but she had to go with her gut instinct when it came to who she allowed near her children. And her gut had told her Keith wasn't the kind of man they could trust.

But Brady Nichols might be. Brady was calm and steady… What would it be like to be with someone whose mood she didn't have to gauge constantly? Her relationship with Mark had been explosive from the start. She'd been young and mistook their pent-up energy for passion. She didn't realize he was simply an angry, disappointed man until it was too late. And Keith, a man who had every reason to be content with his life, seemed to always be grasping. He wanted more than she could give him, and when she refused, he decided to take it.

A burst of radio static interrupted her thoughts, and she whirled to face the older man. He had been careful to keep his communications with his team away from her, but she'd heard Dillon's excited report: "Winnie's got something. Brady and Cal are tracking her. Bentley has an injured paw. We're heading to base."

"I'll radio Jenny and ask her to call Dr. Beaumont

or Tashya to meet us here and take a look at Bentley. Easy does it heading in."

"What? What docs Winnie have?" Cassie demanded when he finished transmitting the call.

"I have no idea," Chief Walters replied calmly.

He glanced down at his phone, and she saw two blue dots moving across the screen from left to right. "Is it them?" she demanded. "Where is she headed? Are they coming this way or arc they moving away from us?" she asked, peering over his arm.

"The dots are Cal and Brady," he corrected. "Winnie and Ruby are out in front of them."

"What did he mean Winnie had something?"

"They are heading slightly closer, but mostly east, which is good. The terrain is much easier."

"East of the mountain? Toward thc rivcr?"

"Not far," he said gruffly. "But in the general direction. Excuse me, I need to make a call," he said, then stepped away, giving her his back to make it clear he wouldn't be answering any more questions.

Cassie twisted her fingers into a cat's cradle of worry, but stuck close to the chief as he radioed dispatch to put in the call for veterinary services.

"Nichols, what's your status?"

A tense minute passed, but at last Brady's breathless reply came with a crackle of static. "In pursuit, sir. Wish I had four legs and about half my height. Winnie's plowing through like a brush cutter."

"Keep us updated."

Cassie moved closer to the chief, heedless of allowing thc man any personal space as they watched the dots moving across the screen, then head toward the bottom.

"Coming this way," he murmured. "Bet they're following Spring Creek."

"Spring Creek?" Cassie repeated, trying to conjure the area maps she'd been studying in preparation for her job as a guide for Blaze's River Tours and Rafting. "It feeds into the Salmon River, right?"

He nodded. "Most creeks in this area do. Spring is mostly fed by snowmelt. It's summer now, so it shouldn't be much more than a few inches deep, but since it's on the northeast side of the hills, it stays wet most of the year."

A crackle of static erupted from his radio, but then nothing followed.

"Should they be done this soon? What does it mean if they're heading in? Do the dogs need to rest or something?" She paced as she fired question after question at the man. "I mean, they'd radio if they'd found them, so this is probably not good news, right?"

"They aren't necessarily headed for base," the chief told her, but he kept his gaze locked on the screen.

Minutes passed, tense and silent. Then they saw the blue dots pause in one spot and hover. "What does it mean when they aren't moving?" she demanded.

"Could be they found something. Could be a waterbreak," he answered tiredly. Then he stabbed at the screen with one blunt fingertip. "Diaz is almost here. We'll see what he has to say." They both swiveled in the direction Dillon's dot indicated, but he didn't appear. When she leaned in closer to peer at the phone, he stepped away and shot her a warning glance. "Get any closer, and people will start to talk."

"Sorry," she whispered. Cassie forced herself to close

her eyes and draw a deep breath. "I'm sorry," she repeated, feeling marginally calmer. "It's been hours."

He gave her shoulder a none-too-gentle pat. "There's a lot of ground to cover. Believe me, you want them to be as thorough as possible."

"I'm sorry. I'm…" she trailed off, completely at a loss to explain her emotional state.

"Keyed up," he provided. "Like I told you, they are the best," he said reassuringly.

"I appreciate everything you all are doing. I hope you know I do," she hastened to add.

"It's our job, ma'am, but even if it weren't we'd be out there. We're going to find your girls." He frowned at the blue dot representing Dillon Diaz. "Diaz should have been here by now. Sometimes, the GPS can lag out here," he explained. "Hard to get an exact bead on them."

Static came through the speaker again, but once more only silence followed. The crunch of gravel and dirt announced the arrival of another vehicle. Parked behind the others, Tashya Pratt climbed out of a Jeep, a jam-packed duffel bag with a veterinary caduceus emblazoned on the side.

"I hear Bentley is hurt," she called to them as she approached, her long legs eating ground. "Doc Beaumont had an emergency at the clinic, but I can help."

Seconds later, Dillon crashed through the brush behind them, his dog, Bentley, cradled in his arms. "Here," Dillon gasped. "And remind me to buy him the diet dog food," he said, sagging as he came toward them with the fluffy Australian shepherd.

Tashya returned Bentley's good-natured doggy grin.

"He's not a bit overweight, are you, B.?" she cooed as Dillon deposited the dog on the open tailgate of the nearest JPD vehicle. "No, you are perfect, aren't you, boy?" she said, her hands moving over the fluffy dog.

Cassie watched as the young woman confidently checked the dog from head to tail.

"It's his right front paw," Dillon said. "Cut on a sharp rock, but possibly sprained or a broken bone."

"I will get to his paws," Tashya said in a singsong tone. She stroked her hands down Bentley's hip and cooed encouragingly to the panting dog. "Give a man a dog, and he thinks he's a vet tech," she teased.

"I know my dog," Dillon grumbled, but gave Tashya the room she needed to go through her routine.

When she did get to the Aussie's right front paw, Bentley gave a sharp yelp to indicate his partner hadn't been wrong. Cassie found herself wanting to add her own soothing coos to Tashya's, but a barrage of insistent barking filled the air.

Dillon's head swiveled. "That's Ruby," he said, spinning in the direction of the barking.

Chief Walters looked down at his phone and then gave it a frustrated shake. "GPS must have been frozen."

"It's not a magic eight ball, Chief," Dillon said, smirking at his boss's insistent shaking.

Before either of the men could stop her, Cassie stumbled out from behind the vehicle and took off in the direction of Ruby's barks.

"Ma'am—" the chief called after her.

"Cassie," Dillon shouted.

Shaking her head in refusal to heed their warnings, she stumbled over rocks and roots, then paused when she heard movement to her left, but all she saw was a flash of light blue that was quickly swallowed by the greenery surrounding her.

She plowed headlong into the brush, heedless of the branches and twigs tearing at her clothing. They found them. Cassie knew it in her gut. She knew it in her heart. She knew her daughters were with Cal and Brady and their dogs, and she wasn't going to wait one second longer to see their faces.

Another short burst of barking made her course correct a little to her right, and she shouted with all her might. "Brooklyn! Jillian!" She knew her babies probably couldn't hear her, but she needed to say their names aloud.

Another round of barking ensued, these ones deeper, more growly and not as sharp as the others. It had to be Winnie.

Something surged through the dense growth behind her, and she jumped and whirled. Dillon Diaz glared at her in disbelief. "You can't go running off into a search scene," he chastised.

"They've got them. I can feel it. I need to get to my girls," she insisted as she took a step away from the glowering officer.

"They've got them, but whoever took them could get you," Dillon argued.

Winnie barked again, and when Cassie swung her head in that direction, she saw two dark-clad figures moving through the woods.

"The GPS and the radio relay were sketchy where they were at," Dillon explained. "Brady's report came through the second after you took off."

Cassie barely heard a word of Dillon's explanation. Frankly, she didn't care. All she wanted to hear was her children's voices. "Brooklyn! Jillian!" she cried again.

"Mommy! Mama!" the girls chorused in reply.

When their voices touched her ears, she crumpled to the soft leaf-mulched ground. "Oh, my God," she whispered. "Oh, thank God."

Behind her, Dillon let out a sharp whistle, and seconds later the two men appeared, each holding a dirt-smudged blonde. Jilly clung to Brady's neck like a koala, but more surprisingly, Brook had abandoned her usual reserve in favor of snuggling Cal. She lifted her head from his shoulder as they came into a small clearing.

"Mommy," she croaked.

Cassie stumbled to her feet and ran toward them. "Are you hurt? Are they hurt?" she demanded, looking from the girls to the men. "Oh, my poor babies," she said in a rush. She pressed a kiss first to Jilly's forehead, then to Brook's. Her elder daughter didn't shy away from the affection as she had so often lately, which troubled Cassie almost as much as it thrilled her. Both girls lunged for her, nearly toppling Cassie, Brady and Cal to the ground in their exuberance.

Jilly slipped into her arms and Cal adjusted his hold on Brook enough to allow her to lean in close. Cassie couldn't stop squeezing them both, needing to confirm they were real and not some wishful thinking she'd conjured.

"Mommy, Winnie and Ruby finded us," Jilly reported, nearly shouting in her excitement. Her daughter glanced over at the dogs standing beside their partners, hero worship written all over her face. "We were by the river and they found us," she continued. Then she wrinkled her freckled nose. "Winnie and Ruby had to sniff my sock. So gross!"

"Your socks are gross," Brook inserted weakly.

"Your socks are perfect. Beautiful." Cassie swiveled her head from one girl to the other, pressing fervent kisses to their grubby cheeks.

From behind her, Brady said, "They both appear to be unharmed, but they were out all night, so we should get them to the hospital for a thorough checkup. They stayed in the cave where I found Jilly's stuff. Brook says Norton took off this morning and never came back."

"I dinnent like him," Jilly announced.

"Me either," Brook chimed in,

"He said I talked too much. Brady's my boyfriend," Jilly said, gazing over at the surprised man adoringly. "He doesn't think I talk too much. I'm gonna marry him and live with Winnie. Brookie can marry Cal."

"I'm already married." Cal chuckled as he shifted Brook's weight. "Besides, I suspect you ladies might only want us for our dogs," he said dejectedly.

Serious as ever, Brook shook her head. "We can be friends," she said solemnly.

Cal beamed at the girl in his arms. "I'd like to be your friend, Miss Brooklyn. Now, let's get you down to one of the cars so your mama can have a good look at you." Cassie babbled her thanks as she followed them, but Cal brushed her gratitude off.

"It's our job, ma'am." Cal answered with a good-natured smile. They all pushed their way through the trees to get to the lane.

Brady jiggled Jilly to get her attention again as he

passed the abandoned pickup, his gazed fixed on the chief's car, which was parked in the rear and off to the side. "If you ask real nice, I bet Chief Walters will put the swirling lights on when he drives you into town."

Confident her eldest was in good hands, Cassie quick-stepped to keep up with them. She gasped when Brady halted suddenly and she found herself standing too close. She looked into his warm brown eyes, but failed to find words good enough to express her thanks.

"Brady, I—"

Wordlessly, he shook his head, then took Jilly from her. "Let's get them to the ER so the docs can have a look. I'll follow you down, and fill you in on what we found." Brady caught Chief Walters's eye. "Sir? Can we get someone here to watch this truck? We couldn't find any signs of Norton, but the girls confirmed he was the one who took them from the party."

The older man reached for his radio. "I'll call down and get the rookie—uh, I mean Jason—to come this way to surveil the truck. Dillon's going to follow Tashya to the veterinary clinic."

"Looks like it's a cut on his paw," she called out to the group. "But I want to get an X-ray to be certain there's no break."

"Thanks, Chief. Cal's going to start the report. I'll be in to add to it once I get statements from Cassie and the girls."

"Sounds like we have a plan." Chief Walters raised a hand and waved it in a circle. "Saddle up. We need to get everyone seen to, and I need to let those federal agents know the girls have been found."

Chapter Twelve

The doctors wanted to keep the girls overnight for observation, to be sure there were no adverse effects of their exposure to the elements. Cassie thanked God this had happened in June, and not January. She hadn't left their side until both girls had dozed off and Aunt Vera came in to sit with them.

"Brady Nichols is sittin' in a chair out in the hall," Vera informed her in as hushed a tone as she could manage. "Looks like he's been dragged behind a horse for a few miles."

She knew he'd been waiting to fill her in and to get her take on things away from impressionable ears, but she hadn't been able to tear herself from her girls. Drawing a deep breath, Cassie rose. She needed to talk to Brady, but she didn't want either of the girls to wake and find anyone but her at their bedside.

"Will you stay with the girls while I go talk to him?" she whispered.

Vera set her purse down. "I drove your van over. Millard will be around in a half hour to get me." With an expression of distaste, she eyeballed the plastic container of salad one of the nurses had brought to her. "I should have thought to bring food. Funny how it's always the last thing on my mind."

"Probably because you look at it all day." Cassie waved her aunt's concern away. "I'm too tired to taste anything anyway. Let me go out to talk to Brady, then I'm going to hit the hay."

Cassie slipped into the corridor, careful to close the door silently behind her. Her heart melted when she took in the sight of Brady sitting in a hard molded-plastic chair. Like the girls, he and Cal had straggled out of the woods dirty and decidedly worse for wear. But Brook and Jilly had been bathed, and patched and outfitted with fresh hospital gowns and socks with non-skid treads.

Vera hadn't been wrong in her assessment. Brady still wore the uniform he'd set out in early that morning. His beard looked thicker after only a day's growth, and his short hair was rumpled. He sat with his eyes closed, his hands laced loosely in his lap and his head tipped against the wall. But something about his posture and breathing told her he wasn't sleeping.

He stirred when she slipped into the seat beside his. Without thinking, she reached over and pulled one of his hands from his lap and squeezed it tightly between hers. It was hard to believe she'd met this man less than forty-eight hours earlier. She already trusted him more than most anyone she knew.

"Brady," she whispered, choked with emotion.

He didn't withdraw his hand, but he did sit straighter in his seat. "How are they?"

"Sleeping," she reported. "You should be too."

"I wanted to talk to you," he said hoarsely.

"You're exhausted," she said, chafing his hand between hers. "We can talk later," she promised.

He shook his head. "I need to fill you in on what we found."

She felt the corners of her lips twitch but kept her expression serious as she asked, "You don't think the girls have filled me in enough? They spent the night in a cave. He left them there alone."

He ducked his head and checked his notes. "I know. But I also want to make sure you have some other facts right."

"The facts can wait until you get a few hours of sleep. Besides, don't you have a report to complete?"

"I dictated most of what I had to say into a voice memo and sent it to Cal. The chief said I could fill in any other blanks and proof the report tomorrow."

"The chief is a smart man." She realized she was still holding his hand and let go of him with a self-conscious laugh. "Sorry."

Brady flexed his fingers. "Nothing to be sorry about."

"Any word on Keith?" she asked, both anxious and hopeful.

The downward turn of Brady's mouth told her there was word, and it wasn't good.

OF COURSE, SHE'D ASKED the question he'd been dreading straight out of the box. His stomach sank, and any pleasure he might have found in her touch was extinguished like a match dropped into a bucket of water.

"I'm sorry to tell you this, but sometime between when we left the scene and when our officer got there, the truck was gone." He sighed. "We can only assume it was Norton. We were already spread thin with three of us on the search. He must have been watching us from someplace in the woods, waiting for a window of opportunity," he said. "We put out an APB to all the surrounding counties and fed the information on the truck to the Jasper grapevine. If he's still in the area, no one has seen him."

Cassie gazed at him in open-mouthed shock, then snapped her jaw shut. "I can't believe he got away."

Brady grimaced and gave a helpless shrug. "I'm sorry. We're not a big department, and we have limited resources." He scrubbed a tired hand over his face, but the minute he let it fall, Cassie reclaimed it, sandwiching it between both of hers once more.

"Don't you dare apologize to me. Don't you dare," she ordered.

"Everybody around here is going to do everything possible to catch this guy and get him put away. Vera and Millard have printed off the picture you gave me, and they're distributing it from the diner. They've made copies, and every business in town is handing them out like candy."

Cassie sucked in a sharp breath. "Oh, my God. I can't believe people are doing all this."

"It's a small town. Everyone wants to help. We got sloppy thinking he wouldn't come for the truck at the first opportunity. We should have made sure there was no gap in the surveillance. I promise you it's not going to happen again."

Cassie let out a startled laugh of disbelief. "You did what you could do."

"Still, it's not safe for you and the girls until we find him."

"It's not like you can post an officer on me 24/7," she said, weariness heavy in her tone.

"Maybe, maybe not. Either way, this part of the hospital stays too busy for him to approach you here. Even if he did, one of the federal agents is sticking close by," he said, nodding to a brawny man dressed in navy blue trousers and a white shirt. He leaned against the counter of the nurses' station, but his eyes were alert.

"He's going to want to talk to the girls. Since this was an abduction, it technically falls under federal jurisdiction. He's going to need to ask a few questions to be able to update things on his end. In the meantime, they've cleared him to hang around the hospital until morning. We'll take the watch from there."

"Okay," Cassie said hesitantly. "But I'm not going to wake the girls so he can talk to them tonight. If they wake up, I'll get him, but until then he's going to have to wait."

"I think we're all good with letting them sleep," Brady said. He waved to the other man, and the agent came over. "Agent Westley Sims, this is Cassie Whitaker. She's Brooklyn and Jillian's mother."

The agent pulled his identification from his pocket and held it out for Cassie to inspect. "I'm terribly sorry for your trouble, ma'am. I understand the girls are resting now. I'm going to stay here overnight, and if anytime in those hours you see fit to let me have a few words with them, I sure would appreciate it. I need to touch base with Boise first thing tomorrow and coordinate with the local authorities in the search for Mr. Norton."

Cassie gave him cordial nod. "It's nice to meet you, and thank you for not asking me to wake them. I figure they're probably going to be out until after suppertime, but I doubt they make it through the night." She shrugged. "They may not have slept at all last night."

The agent inclined his head. "I won't ask you to wake them until tomorrow morning if they don't come around on their own. Sound reasonable?"

"Yes, thank you. More than reasonable." She looked at Brady, seemingly oblivious to the fact she still held his hand between both of hers. "You and I can talk later. I really want you to go home and get some rest. They're going to put a cot for me in the room with the girls, and I don't plan on budging again." She gave a choked laugh. "Heck, I may not let them out of my sight until their eighteenth birthdays. Maybe not ever."

"No one could blame you," Brady reassured her. Reluctantly, he extracted his hand from hers and rose from the chair with a groan. "Okay. I'm heading home to take a hot shower and try to catch a few hours of sleep myself. You have my number in your phone. Call for any reason at all."

Cassie pressed her lips together to stifle a protest, but said only, "I will. I promise."

Brady gestured to the chair, then at Agent Sims. "If I were you, I'd try to sweet-talk one of the nurses into a spare desk chair. These things could be used as instruments of torture."

The federal agent smirked. "I've got more experience at sweet-talking nurses and kidnapping cases than you have scruffy whiskers. Don't you worry about me."

Cassie stood too, then gazed at the floor, her forehead puckering. "Where's Winnie?"

"Dillon has her at his house."

Her hand flew to her mouth. "I forgot to ask how Bentley is," she said, clearly horrified.

Brady shuffled. "You may have had a thing or two on your mind. Bentley's fine. Got a cut on his paw and lost a toenail. Nothing broken."

"Oh, poor baby," she said in a rush.

Warmed by her unabashed affection for the animals, Brady inclined his head. "He's going to be okay. We're all going to be okay."

With a nod, Agent Sims returned to the nurses' station to give them some space. Grateful for the man's circumspection, Brady reached for Cassie's hand and held it between both of his. "Promise me you'll call if anything spooks you," he insisted. "Anything at all."

"Promise me you'll sleep," she countered. "You can text me in the morning."

He released her hand. He drew a deep breath as he pulled away, summoning the power to set his body in motion again. "Okay. I am going to sleep, but only because you want me to."

Cassie laughed out loud, the sound of it bouncing off the sterile walls of the hospital corridor. "I also want a cheeseburger. Can you make one appear?"

Brady made a show of searching his pockets and patting down the utility vest he still wore. "Darn, I'm fresh out of cheeseburgers."

"Looks like I'm gonna have to eat the salad they

brought from the cafeteria for me," Cassie said mournfully. "Good night, Lieutenant Nichols. Sleep well."

Brady turned on his heel, unoffended by her dismissal. He was dead on his feet. Pulling his phone from his pocket, he tapped the screen until Dillon's number appeared. When his friend answered, he asked, "Can you handle one more houseguest tonight? I don't think I can drive all the way out to my place."

Dillon murmured something to one of the dogs, then replied. "Sure, no problem, man. You hungry?"

"Starving."

"I threw a couple burgers on the grill. I think we deserve a double after the day we've had. I can throw a couple more on," Dillon offered.

Brady stopped outside the sliding doors and looked at the hospital facade. "Can you make about three more, and are you willing to deliver?"

Chapter Thirteen

A knock startled her awake, and Cassie rubbed the sleep from her eyes and saw Agent Sims poke his head through the door. She started to rise to greet him, but found both girls had crawled onto the rollaway cot with her at some point during the night.

"I'm sorry to wake you," he whispered, "but I really do need to take a statement, and they're starting to bring breakfast trays around."

She waved in acknowledgment, then glanced at the girls snuggled into her. "Give us fifteen minutes."

In those precious few minutes, she managed to rouse the groggy girls and herd them into the adjoining bathroom. Faces washed, teeth brushed and hair combed, they were ready to entertain guests. A woman with a volunteer tag clipped to her scrubs bustled in carrying two covered trays stacked one on top of the other.

Brook and Jilly returned to their beds, but the novelty of being served a meal on a rolling table had been exhausted the night before. Their excited chatter had died away too. She watched as Brook prodded the pale scrambled eggs with her fork, and Jilly waved a limp piece of bacon, trying to make it fly like a bird flapping its wings. It was painfully obvious Jilly didn't have it in her to really sell her stunt.

Sighing, Cassie pushed aside the cot she'd folded in half and secured with a strap to the side and dragged a chair between the beds. "Girls, there's a man here—"

Brook dropped her fork with a clatter, and Jilly stopped flapping the strip of bacon. "What man?" her youngest asked with uncharacteristic wariness.

Cassie's heart squeezed. Would they ever be able to recapture what innocence they had before Keith Norton upended their world? Would any of them ever feel safe again? She hated him for stealing her daughters from her, but would resent him for the rest of her life for snatching their innocence away too.

"A nice man," Cassie said, calm and cool, though she seethed inside. "His name is Agent Sims, and he wants to talk to us all about what happened."

"I don't want to talk about it anymore," Brook said, her expression turning mulish.

"His name is Agent?" Jilly asked, her expression perplexed. "I've never met anybody named Agent."

Cassie shut her eyes and inhaled deeply, counting to three as she exhaled. "No, agent is not his name. It's his job. Like Officer Nichols, or Dr. Beaumont. He's a special agent with a, uh, place called the Federal Bureau of Investigation. When someone takes a kid without asking their mommy if it's okay first, they help look for them," she explained.

"But Brady already finded us," Jilly pointed out.

"And we talked to Brady's boss guy," Brook chimed in, her jaw still set.

"Yes, well, they work for a different place and had

to get their own story. Now, Agent Sims wants to hear your story."

Brook narrowed her eyes mutinously. "What if we don't want to tell it again?"

Cassie reached over and snatched a piece of cold toast from her daughter's tray. "Sometimes we have to do things we don't want to do," she said, relying on a familiar refrain.

Jilly caught on right away "Like clean our room," she said, dropping the hapless bacon onto her plate.

"Exactly." Cassie devoured the triangle of toast in two more bites as she walked to the door. Holding on to the handle while she chewed, she fixed the girls with her I-mean-business stare. "We're going to be helpful and polite to Agent Sims, then I will text Officer Brady and tell him we're ready to go home."

The interview with Special Agent Westley Sims didn't take long. He covered much of the same ground Chief Walters, Cal and Brady had, but in a much more direct way. The girls chafed against answering more questions at first, but soon warmed to sharing the dramatic tale of their rescue again. Cassie looked forward to telling Brady and Cal they had achieved superhero status as far as her daughters were concerned.

Sims pressed the button to stop the recording he'd made of their interview, and Cassie stood. She only intended to see the FBI agent to the door, but at a jerk of his head, he indicated he wanted her to follow him into the corridor.

"We're searching for Keith Norton. The temporary tag on the truck seems to be registered to a woman named Marcia Thomas. Does the name ring a bell?"

Stunned, Cassie's jaw dropped. "Uh, yes." She swallowed hard, then cleared her throat. "Yes, um, Marcia is the office manager at Bozeman Dental, the practice where Keith works."

Agent Sims put his phone away and pulled out a notebook. "There's the connection we need." He closed the notebook, then shoved it into the same pocket as his phone. He ran a hand over his face, and it occurred to her he had stayed awake all night watching over them. "Do you mind passing the information along to the locals?" he asked, gesturing toward the double doors at the end of the hall. "I'd like to get on the road."

She looked to find Brady Nichols striding toward her. He wore a uniform, but not tactical gear. "No, I... Yes, fine. Please," she stammered as an unexpected wave of relief pulsed through her. "Is it safe for you to drive?"

The other man waved her concern away. "I've got a few more hours in me." He rose when Brady approached. "I'll be hitting the road, but I'll be in touch." He offered his hand to her first, then moved to Brady and did the same.

"Thanks for your help on this," Brady replied.

Cassie waited until he left, then shifted her attention back to Brady, her mind racing with the information about the truck, unable to parse out the exact nature of Marcia and Keith's relationship. "The temporary tags on the truck are registered to a woman who works in Keith's office," she blurted.

He inclined his head. "Marcia Thomas," he confirmed. "We've already got someone from Bozeman PD heading out to talk to her."

She shook her head, boggled. "Marcia is..."

Brady watched her carefully. "Involved with Norton?" he prompted when she stalled out.

"Old enough to be his mother," she said, wide-eyed. "She's married. A grandmother. Leads a Sunday school class." She frowned as she tried to work it all out in her mind. "Do you think he stole the truck from her? I don't remember Marcia driving a pickup, but I didn't work there long." She wrinkled her nose, trying as hard as she might to make the pieces fit. "She's not really the truck type." He looked at her quizzically, and she shrugged. "Older woman, wears lots of floral dresses, drinks hot tea year-round."

"And do you think she has a thing for Norton?" Brady asked.

"A thing?" Cassie grimaced. "Not like a crush. More of a sort of hero worship. She thinks anyone with Doctor in front of their name walks on water."

"But he's not exactly the kind of doctor who saves people's lives," Brady said dryly.

"I don't think she makes the distinction." Cassie shrugged. "For some people it's all about the title and prestige." She waved a hand toward the door of the hospital room. "Speaking of prestige, your fan club is waiting for you."

"Fan club? Are you telling me I made a good impression?"

"Only slightly less than godlike. They wanted me to give them my phone this morning so they could order capes for you and Cal," Cassie said, fixing him with a droll stare.

"Capes?"

"Because you're superheroes," she explained. "Anybody who saves anybody is worthy of the title as far as the under-ten crowd is concerned."

He flashed a self-deprecating smirk. "If only it worked so well with the over-ten crowd."

She rolled her eyes and reached for the door handle. "I doubt you have any trouble, Lieutenant."

Both girls cried out with pleasure upon seeing Brady follow her into their room. Cassie stood nearby and watched as he answered their rapid-fire questions concerning his whereabouts, and what Winnie, Ruby and every single one of the other people they'd met from the search team were doing. He held his own under the interrogation.

It wasn't until Brook fell silent, allowing her younger sister to continue the barrage, that Cassie's maternal radar pinged. When there was a pause for breath, her older daughter asked the question uppermost on everyone's minds.

"Did you catch the bad guy?"

There was a beat of charged silence, then Brady gave his head a slow shake. "Not yet, but we will."

Brook's stare was a mixture of apprehension and speculation. His answer even put a damper on Jilly's enthusiasm, but Cassie wasn't as worried for her. Her baby always bounced back quickly. Brady looked around, clearly at a loss. Feeling bad for him, Cassie diverted the conversation.

"So, we're waiting for the doctor to tell us we can go home. We all had a good night's rest, and we hope you did too, don't we, girls?" she prodded.

They each dutifully answered with a mumbled "yes,

ma'am," but the previous jubilation filling the room had lessened considerably.

As Cassie searched for a neutral topic, Brady swung around to face her. "Did you get my delivery last night? I was too shot to do anything but snarf one down for myself and fall face-first onto Dillon's foldout couch."

Cassie recalled how good it felt to fall asleep with a full belly, a warm blanket and the soft sighs of her daughters surrounding her. The rollaway cot was nothing to write home about, but compared to a night of worrying and wondering, it was as plush as a cloud.

"Yes, thank you. It was exactly what I needed." She touched his arm. "And please thank Dillon for me too. I was half asleep when he came in, and I have no clue if I even said thank-you. I pounced on the burger like I was feral, though."

He grinned. "We're glad to be of service," he replied.

"I'll tell Vera you two get breakfast on me when you visit the diner."

"Not necessary." He shifted nervously from foot to foot. Cassie got the distinct impression he wanted to be anywhere but standing in their hospital room. Figuring she needed to let him off the hook, she gave his arm one last squeeze. "Thank you for coming by to check on us. My aunt dropped the van off, so as soon as the doctor clears us, we'll be by the station to finish anything you need, then head home."

He tipped his head to the side, debating whether he should speak his mind. Feeling they were well beyond any pretense, Cassie mimicked his tilted head and asked, "Was there something you wanted?"

"Listen, I don't want to overstep any bounds or anything, and this might sound kind of, um, sexist? But I don't mean it to come across that way."

"Well, now I'm intrigued," she said, crossing her arms over her chest. "What's on your mind?"

"I was thinking I would feel better, and hopefully you would feel better, if maybe I…" He trailed off and rubbed the nape of his neck in a fidgety, vulnerable way. The uneasy movements made her soften inside. Then he inclined his head toward the door, indicating they should step away from the girls to speak more privately.

She followed him. "What is it?"

"I guess I was thinking I could go by your house and check to make sure everything is secure, I mean with your permission." He shoved his hands into the pockets of his uniform pants. "People have been keeping an eye out for Norton's truck, but I'm not sure anyone's going to check the property itself to see if he's been around there," he said in a low voice.

Cassie blinked. She'd been so relieved to see the girls, she hadn't thought much about the continued threat to their safety. "Yes. Please. If you don't mind," she hastened to add.

"I wouldn't have offered if I didn't mean it," Brady reassured her. "I'll go by there now and meet you at the station." Turning to the girls, he called out, "I gotta go. Winnie is pretty jealous if I talk to other girls for too long."

Both Brook and Jilly laughed, but Cassie could hear the hollowness in their giggles. It made her chest ache and filled her with a righteous fury she wished she could rain down on Keith Norton. He'd not only stolen her girls, but he'd also taken away the precious safety and security they'd sought here in Jasper. She hadn't done anything to deserve this. Her girls certainly hadn't done anything to warrant having their lives risked and the possible trauma from this experience. And what did he think would happen between them? Did the man actually believe this was the way to get in good with her? Was she supposed to pack up her kids, move back to Montana, and date the man who stole her babies? Oh no. Never in a million years. If he thought she'd have anything to do with him after what he'd put them through, he was sadly mistaken. No, the police would find Keith Norton, and he'd better hope the law got to him before she did.

Chapter Fourteen

The door had barely closed behind Brady when Adele, the nurse on the morning shift, came bustling in wearing scrubs printed with cats holding umbrellas and dogs tumbling from the sky. The girls' displeasure in Brady leaving was quickly forgotten when faced with such fabulous fashion sense. Cassie dropped into the chair and heaved a sigh, wishing this whole nightmare could end so she could simply take her daughters and go home.

Adele ran through her tasks with brisk efficiency, then cheerfully informed them Dr. Stenz was on duty this morning and making his rounds now. Not long after, a grandfatherly man with a shock of white hair and half-moon-shaped reading glasses came in to give the girls one last going-over as he signed their release papers.

But they weren't done yet. A social worker stopped by to speak to the girls about their experience, then provided Cassie with a printed list of resources available to kids who had suffered a traumatic event. They were wrapping the interview when Cassie received a call from Agent Sims wanting to clarify she had definitely never seen the pickup truck Norton left parked in the fire lane leading into the woods.

Then Chief Walters made his entrance.

But rather than bringing news or hammering them with questions, he simply grinned at the fresh-faced girls. "I thought I might escort the ladies of the hour to their car."

Brook and Jilly preened as they were loaded into wheelchairs, peppering the chief on whether he had a dog, and if so, why didn't his dog go to work with him? He told them he did, but Bruno was an old hound who'd flunked out of the Daniels Canine Academy after wandering off one too many times, so he now spent his days keeping a watchful eye on the chief's refrigerator.

The two nurses pushing the chairs parked them near the sliding glass doors with a flourish. They waited under the watchful gaze of Chief Walters until Cassie brought her van around. Once the girls were buckled in, she thanked the chief again for all he and his team had done to recover her daughters. But the grim expression on the older man's face as he gazed at the screen of his phone stopped her.

"What is it?" she demanded without preamble.

His head jerked. "What makes you think it has anything to do with you, Ms. Whitaker?" He gave her a wry smile to soften the rebuke. "I am responsible for the whole town, not just you, ma'am."

A hot, prickly rush of embarrassment crept up her throat and made the tips of her ears burn. "I'm sorry," she responded quickly. "I guess I'm in my own bubble," she said, gesturing to the van and their immediate vicinity. "Trust me, I understand not everything is about me."

He stepped away. "You've been through a lot these last few days. I think I can forgive you a smidge of self-absorption," he said, his eyes narrowing and his lips curving into a teasing grin.

"I do appreciate everything you've done." Cassie lifted her hand in a wave.

"Don't forget to go by the station on your way home," he reminded her. "I know you're all tired of being questioned and prodded, but I'm sure at least one or two of the dogs will be there."

"That's all they'll need to hear," she assured him as she climbed into the driver's seat. "Thank you again. I can't thank you enough."

The chief touched the brim of his hat like a cowboy in an old Western. "Just doing my job, ma'am."

On a laugh, Cassie slammed the car door and started the engine. They hadn't even made it out of the hospital parking lot when the girls began bickering. What would have annoyed her two or three days ago now sounded like sweet music to her ears. In the cup holder her phone buzzed, and she saw a text notification, but she refused to check while driving. Her old van wasn't equipped with all the latest technology, so whatever it was would have to wait.

The girls were at it full tilt when she swung into the parking lot adjacent to the Jasper Police Department. She parked in the same spot, but it felt like months had passed rather than days. She switched off the engine, and their complaints with one another morphed into groans of tired frustration.

"Why can't we go home?" Jilly whined.

"How many people do we have to tell?" Brook asked

derisively. "Can't one person write it down and pass it on to everybody else?"

"No, I'm afraid not," Cassie commiserated. Then she whipped out another tried-and-true mom line. "Sorry, chickees. I don't make the rules—I only follow them."

She climbed out of the van, grateful the lame momism seemed to work. Brook unhooked her seat belt the second Cassie slid the door open, but Jilly, annoyed she was still required to use a booster on her seat due to being slightly underweight for her age, remained stubbornly strapped in.

She claimed that if she was so small she had to sit in a baby seat, then she was too much of a baby to unbuckle her own seat belt. Most days they argued about it, but today, Cassie was almost pathetically happy to unclip it for her.

Loath to let either of the girls stray too far from her, she planted a hand on their heads and playfully propelled them toward the front of the station. Once they stumbled through the glass doors, the three of them were laughing again.

A woman at the front desk beamed at them. "Well, there they are! You girls are practically celebrities around here," she said, clapping her hands together and coming out from behind her desk. Turning to Cassie, she spoke in a hushed tone. "I'm Teresa Norwood. I've worked here since dinosaurs walked the earth, and I've never… Well, that doesn't matter. I can't tell you how happy we all are to see your girls safe. Thank goodness." Turning to the girls, she leaned down. "Would anyone like a cup of cocoa?"

Almost in unison, the girls answered with a murmured "yes." Brook added a polite "please," and Jilly belatedly tacked on a whispered "ma'am" at the end.

Teresa gestured for the girls to follow her. "Oh, you don't have to 'ma'am' me, sweetheart. You can call me Miss T. Everybody else does. Now, who here likes cinnamon rolls?" When the girls' faces brightened, she shot Cassie a questioning glance. Not looking abashed for failing to ask permission, but more to ask if she was interested. Cassie's stomach growled, the triangle of toast long forgotten.

"I made some fresh this morning," Teresa said coaxingly. "Do you want one too?"

Cassie nodded enthusiastically. "Oh yes, ma'am, Miss T. I most certainly do."

Teresa tilted her head toward the room where the officers' desks were aligned. "You know which desk is Brady's?" she asked.

Cassie pointed to it, and Teresa beamed again. "Good. You settle yourself in. He radioed our dispatcher, Jenny, a few minutes ago to tell her he was heading in and asked if you could wait for him. You go ahead and have a seat there while the girls and I make sure these rolls are nice and warm."

Cassie was still processing when the older woman stooped to talk to her daughters. "Winnie is going to be beside herself with excitement when she sees you two. You are all she has talked about all morning."

The girls giggled as they followed the older woman into what appeared to be a small break room off the main office.

Cassie made her way to Brady's desk and dropped heavily into the chair beside it. The only other officer in the room was Cal Hoover. He'd given her a wave, then indicated the cell phone wedged against his ear, implying he couldn't talk. Glad to have a minute alone, Cassie closed her eyes and let her chin fall to her chest. More than anything, she wanted to sleep in her own bed. If she could sleep at all.

She practiced the deep breathing exercises the counselor she'd seen in Bozeman had taught her, hoping to center herself. She'd almost made it through her fifth slow inhalation and exhalation when Cal interrupted her brief meditation.

"Marcia Thomas says she has never owned a pickup truck," he announced from across the room.

"I didn't think she was the type," Cassie said, sitting straighter. "Did she say why there are temporary tags in her name on one parked near the spot where my missing daughters were found?"

One side of his mouth curled and he rose from his chair, stretching his long, lanky frame. "As a matter of fact, she did. Turns out, one of the doctors who works at the practice she manages bought it from her brother. He asked if she could handle the registration for him, but she didn't have some of the information she needed, so she put it in her name with the understanding he'd transfer it over when he had a chance."

"And the doctor's name happens to be…" she prompted.

"Keith Norton."

"Shocker." She said the last in a deadpan tone, but inside she was ready to kick the mealymouthed jerk all the way to the Idaho-Montana state line. Or better yet, feed him to the Feds. "I don't suppose she had any idea where we could find Dr. Norton," she said dryly.

Cal gave his head a mournful shake, then stooped to glance at his notes. "No. According to Ms. Thomas, the good doctor is supposed to be visiting his brother in Tacoma this week."

"Keith Norton is an only child," she informed him stonily.

Brady walked through the door, his expression grim. Cassie rose from her seat to go meet him half-way. "What? What's wrong?"

He shook his head and gestured for her to reclaim the chair she'd abandoned. He dropped into his own seat adjacent to hers and laced his hands behind his head, tipping his face to the ceiling.

"This town, man," he muttered. "It's like they're living in some kind of dreamworld where nothing bad ever happens."

Cal smirked. It seemed this was an old refrain.

"What do you mean?" Cassie asked, feeling defensive.

The other officer explained. "Brady likes to rant once a week about how nobody around here locks their doors."

"I do," Cassie said without hesitation. "I lock my doors and my windows."

Brady stared at her with such intensity she wanted to squirm, but she held it together. "You're sure you do? Front and back doors?"

Cassie raised her eyebrows. "Absolutely. A person doesn't go through some of the stuff I've gone through without learning how important basic safety precautions can be," she told him dryly. "I always double-check the doors and windows when I leave, and then lock the front door with my key from the outside."

Brady's interest sharpened. "And you're certain you did on the day of the party?"

"Yes," Cassie spoke emphatically. "As a matter of fact, I had to go in again to find Jilly's shoe. It was on the patio." She glanced at Cal, communicating the sort of understanding you could only find in a fellow parent. "I remember dropping the shoe as I reset the lock on the door." Then the implications of Brady's questioning finally broke through her brain fog. "Why? Was the door unlocked?"

Brady hesitated only briefly, then nodded. "It doesn't look to have been forced, so I assumed you hadn't locked it."

"You assumed wrong."

"What kind of a lock is it?" Cal asked.

Cassie shook her head. "Standard lock on the doorknob. I meant to install something stronger, but I haven't gotten around to it yet."

Brady scribbled something in his ever-present notebook, then said to Cal, "Might be a fairly easy kind of lock to pick," he commented.

When the other officer made note of the observation, Cassie leaned in and added, "Particularly if you're a dentist and used to working with small, precise instruments."

Brady looked around. "Where are the girls?"

"Teresa has them in the break room, pumping them full of cocoa and about twenty pounds of sugar," Cassie reported.

"Would you be open to leaving them here? We can

ask Teresa if she'd mind keeping an eye on them while we head over to the house to see if anything's been disturbed. I didn't go farther than the kitchen because I honestly didn't think we were looking at a possible breaking and entering."

Cassie raised a shoulder. "Sure, if you don't think Teresa would mind."

Brady launched himself from his seat. "It shouldn't take long. I'll go ask her now. And I'll ask the girls to give Winnie a good brushing and rubdown. Tell them she needs some pampering after yesterday's excursions."

"Perfect," she agreed.

Cal backed away. "You'll fill him in on what we discovered about the registration?" he asked Cassie.

"I will." She wrinkled her nose. "I still need to figure out whether I buy her explanation or not. Marcia is a super–straight arrow. I can't imagine her falsifying an official government document."

"Do you think she's covering for him?" Cal asked.

Cassie tossed his question off with a shrug. "Anyone's guess. It's a strange situation. I don't believe she'd say no to anything he asked her to do, because as far as she's concerned, all the doctors walk on water. On the other hand, I can't imagine she did it without qualms." She chewed her lip as she considered the possibility. "She's a by-the-book sort of person. How did she sound on the phone?"

"Nervous," Cal said, his eyes narrowing. "I get what you're saying about not being the type to falsify information. Perhaps she really did think she was doing both her brother and Norton a solid," he answered grimly. "Either way, she did you and your girls no favor."

Cassie stood as Brady emerged from the break room and gave her a thumbs-up.

"I appreciate your due diligence on this," she said to Cal. "It probably is as she said, but maybe she'll think twice about who she trusts. A call from a police officer saying her name was on the registration for a truck used to perpetrate a crime could not have gone over well with her."

Cal chuckled as he resumed his position at his desk. "No. I have to say she was pretty agitated about it."

Brady looked between them quizzically, then hooked a thumb toward the door. "You can fill me in on the way. I want to get this over with and I don't want the girls to get too antsy."

Cassie felt her shoulders drop. It was nice to be around somebody who cared about her girls as much as he did her. "Let's get to it, then."

Chapter Fifteen

Brady parked his SUV a block from Cassie's house. When she looked at him quizzically, he killed the ignition and shrugged. "It's a marked car. I don't want him getting squirrelly if he sees it."

"Squirrelly," she repeated with a laugh. "He hasn't seemed overly worried about the law catching him to this point, but sure, probably a good idea," she conceded.

They walked down the sidewalk in silence, but when they reached her neighbor's house, he indicated they should take a shortcut through Mrs. Garbowski's yard.

Cassie put a hand on his arm to stop him before he could place a foot on the neatly trimmed turf of the woman's lawn. "Mrs. Garbowski doesn't like people walking on her grass," she explained. "She's particular about weird things. If I let mine get above optimal two-inch height, she's after me to mow it."

Brady chuckled. "I discovered most of this earlier, but when I showed her my credentials and explained why it was important for me to cut across her property, she gave her permission."

Cassie snorted, but followed him across the lawn

around the side of the older woman's home and through her backyard. "I can't imagine how much charm and sweet talk you had to pour on to make this happen," she said, eyeballing the other woman's house as they crossed the boundary from her yard onto the slightly more unkempt lawn surrounding Cassie's grandparents' former home.

Brady held out an arm to indicate the invisible property line. "I can't believe there isn't a fence."

"My grandpa wanted to put one in, but Mrs. Garbowski wouldn't agree to fencing her side of the property. He always said there was no point in building one two-thirds of the way around the yard."

Brady laughed. "Nope. Absolutely no point."

Cassie led the way to the shallow back steps, through the screen door and into a small mudroom. They stopped at the door. She hesitated, then reached for the knob and twisted. When it swung open easily, her jaw dropped in disbelief, but she didn't balk.

"We can take a minute if you aren't ready to go in."

She glanced over at him. "What if he's in there?"

Brady rested his hand on the utility belt near his sidearm. "With your permission, I'll do a sweep of the whole house. You can come in once I know it's clear."

Cassie shuddered, then gestured for him to proceed. "By all means, permission granted."

Brady opened the clasp on his belt to withdraw his service weapon. Holding it aloft, he moved through the kitchen, his head swiveling as he took in everything he could. There was a door beside the refrigerator he could only assume led to a pantry. Placing his back against the wood panels, he lowered his gun into position and reached for the knob. He opened it slowly, allowing his firearm to take the lead. It was indeed a pantry, but there were no runaway kidnappers stored in there.

He swept through the living room, his heart rate kicking into overdrive as he took in the barely contained chaos of a home well lived in. A family home. How dare this jerk violate what should have been their safe space?

He moved his way down the hall, poking his head around open doorways, his service revolver blazing the trail. Brady worked methodically, feeling slightly abashed when he whipped around one doorway and found himself pointing his gun at the biggest stuffed unicorn he'd ever seen outside of a county fair.

Brook's room, he guessed, scanning the neat stacks of books and the toys stored in a large plastic bin. He moved on. Sure enough, the next room was a messy mishmash of ballerinas, stuffed dogs, unicorns, of course, and some truly frightening dolls with cartoon-like facial features. Definitely more Jilly's style.

He checked the hall bath next, making sure to pull the shower curtain all the way so he could be certain no one lurked in the tub. Then he moved down to the end of the hall into what appeared to be the master bedroom.

The bed was neatly made. There were few mementos or personal effects scattered around. He imagined Cassie had left whatever bric-a-brac she'd collected in her adult life in Montana, and hadn't had the inclination to fill the room with any more than what she absolutely needed.

A shallow tray on the top of the dresser contained bits and pieces of jewelry and a few hair accessories. The furniture itself was heavy and old-fashioned. He assumed it was left behind by her grandparents, because he certainly couldn't imagine Cassie Whitaker walking into a furniture store and selecting this particular suite.

Lowering his gun a few inches, he made his way over to the en suite bath. A shower framed in trendy 1980s brass and glass made it easy to see the room was clear of unwanted guests. But a ripple ran the length of his spine when he moved to leave and noticed someone had scrawled a warning on the mirror.

It read simply, "I'll be back for you."

Brady eyed the basket of cosmetics on the vanity and retreated, mindful of the need to preserve the scene. "Over my dead body," he muttered.

Spinning on his heel, he stalked through the house to the kitchen, where he found Cassie nervously fiddling with the coffee maker.

She gave him a wobbly smile. "I could use a cup. How about you?"

"No, I think we'd better not," he told her.

"You didn't find anyone hiding under the beds, did you?"

She graced him with a tremulous but hopeful smile. He hated to be the one to wipe it off her face.

"There's nobody currently here, but I can tell you he has been here."

Cassie's hand trembled as she set the plastic scoop she'd been using to fill the coffee filter down on the counter with a thud. Grounds scattered on the laminate countertop. "Are you kidding me?"

"I wish, but I rarely joke about breaking and entering." Brady tried to mask his impatience, but it must have shown on his face, because she shook her head quickly and began sweeping the spilled grounds from the countertop with the side of her hand.

"Right. Of course not," she said. "I can't believe he's been here."

"I'm going to call in a crime scene unit to try to see if he left any fingerprints, but I don't think it's safe for you and the girls to stay here."

"No. Right. Oh, my God," she said, each word reaching for a higher octave.

"Do you think you could stay with Vera and Millard?"

She shrugged. "I'm sure we could. We'll have no choice, really," she said grimly. "I hate to do it to them, though. They keep such early hours, and the girls are so noisy. It's not a good mix. Certainly not any kind of long-term solution, and it's hard to know how long it will take to catch him."

"Hopefully, we won't need long-term, but I understand what you're saying," Brady said with confidence borne of pure determination. "We'll figure out something else. Let me radio this in."

Freeing the mic from his lapel, he pressed the key to open the channel. "Jenny, can you have Cal grab Ruby and head to Cassie Whitaker's place?"

"Cal?" the dispatcher asked, clearly puzzled by the request. "Do you need him to bring Winnie too?"

Brady met Cassie's eyes, then gave his head a slight shake. "Leave Winnie there with Teresa and the Whitaker girls for now. It looks like our suspect may have been on the premises. We'll need a crime scene unit for the interior, and I'd like Cal and Ruby to search the perimeter."

"Ten-four," came the reply from the dispatcher. A crackle of static followed, and then Jenny said, "I'll call the county guys for the forensics. They have a bigger team and can probably get the processing done faster."

"Good thinking. Over."

Brady reattached the microphone to his lapel, then looked down at Cassie. "I think you should gather whatever clothes and other essentials you and the girls need, but I'm going to ask you to touch as little as possible inside the house. I'm aware your prints are all over the place already. We just don't want to risk any overlapping."

Cassie raised a hand to indicate he didn't need to say more. "Gotcha."

She stood in front of him, wringing her hands, her bottom lip caught between her teeth. The urge to wrap her in his arms was nearly overwhelming, but Brady wasn't about to overstep his bounds. Particularly not with a woman who'd been through what she'd been through.

"Maybe I can rent one of the cabins from Blaze's River Tours instead of going to Vera and Millard's." She winced. "Of course, they'd have us if I asked, but we're so disruptive to them. And the girls would be like elephants learning to tiptoe."

"I understand." He jerked his head toward the hallway and said, "Go gather what you need, and we'll think of something. But please don't go in the master bath. If there's anything you need from in there, we'll have to buy it new."

Cassie stared at him, her jaw dropping open. "The bathroom? What did he do?"

"Nothing gruesome," he assured her. "But he left you a message. It's also the one room where we have the best chance of lifting fingerprints since we're fairly sure he was in there touching things," he concluded. "It's only going to be upsetting to you to see it."

Cassie stood straighter. "Shouldn't I be the judge of what I can handle? If the message was left for me, I should see it."

"Trust me on this. He only wants to get into your head." He leveled her with a steady gaze. "Do not let him in."

She eyed him mutinously, then her shoulders sagged. Her quiet "Okay" was more than an acquiescence. With a single word, she told Brady she trusted him. And he was not at all oblivious to what a big issue trust was for her.

"Thank you," he said, inclining his head.

She frowned. "For what?"

"For believing me. If there were something I thought you could decipher or some deeper meaning, I'd take you in there myself, but he's only trying to scare you. Thank you for not giving him the satisfaction."

Cassie gave a short bark of laughter. "Oh, I'm plenty scared," she said as she started down the hall. "Right now, I'm more mad than scared."

Brady followed her as she strode from room to room, packing a small backpack full of clothes for each girl, grabbing their spinning toothbrushes and sparkly toothpaste from the bathroom off the hallway, then finally moving to her own room. Mad was good. He could work with mad. He was glad she wasn't crying again. Watching her cry into his dog's fur tore him to shreds.

He stayed close to her. Not because he didn't trust her not to open the bathroom door he'd so carefully pulled closed, but because he didn't want to let her out of his sight. The realization struck him like a blow. Without thinking, he was about to make an offer with the potential to earn him an honest-to-goodness slap across the face.

"Listen, this might sound…odd, but I have a suggestion."

Cassie paused in the process of pulling a stack of T-shirts from a drawer. "A suggestion?"

"Rather than spending money on a cabin, why don't you and the girls stay out at my place?"

Chapter Sixteen

"Your place?"

Brady grimaced, but he couldn't blame her for the skepticism in her tone. He lifted a hand to stay any immediate protest, then stepped into the room. "I live a few miles outside of town. Not far from the Daniels ranch. I bought a large piece of property out there, and I'm building a house." He rubbed his neck, wondering if it sounded like he was trying to impress her—which he may have been, but that honestly wasn't his motivation. "Right now, I'm living in a double-wide mobile home I bought used. It's kind of dated, but it has three bedrooms. If the girls don't mind sharing, it would be plenty of room."

He paused, trying to gauge her blank expression for any indication of how this might be landing. When she didn't say anything, he went on in a rush.

"Think about it. You would be out of town. We wouldn't tell anybody but your aunt and uncle and the Jasper PD where you were staying. You'd be with a policeman and a trained police dog," he said with a shrug. "What could be safer?"

"What happens when you go on duty?"

Brady pondered the possibilities. He had no doubt in his mind he could convince the chief this plan was a good one. And even if he couldn't, he had plenty of unused leave coming his way. If the department didn't want to go along, he'd take the days off. He needed to put in a few hours working on his house.

"I can figure things out. As a matter of fact, it might be better if you talked to Vera about not taking any shifts for the next few days. I believe Norton is sticking close, and in my opinion, you need to consider keeping a low profile."

"Hiding," she said flatly.

"Better to frame it as keeping yourself and your girls safe," he said gently.

She sighed and her shoulders slumped. Brady knew he'd won the argument, but it didn't feel good. Rather than gloating, he focused on logistics.

"What's your schedule looking like with Blaze's?"

She shrugged. "I pretty much go in whenever I am free. I'm a trainee, and an hourly employee. Since I can't take any tours out alone, I wouldn't be messing with anyone's schedule but my own."

Brady searched her expression for a hint of wariness about him. "See? It's a good plan. You and the girls need to disappear for a few days. We can even put it about town he got scared and moved on." When she tipped her chin stubbornly, he pressed gently. "I'm not saying you should, but gossip spreads like brush fire around here. A whisper or two in case Norton is listening in somewhere."

"For the record, I didn't leave Bozeman because I was scared of Keith Norton. And I didn't leave Billings because I was scared of my ex-husband. I moved on because I want to live my life and raise my girls in a place we feel safe and secure. But I don't run away because I'm scared. I'm tired of men trying to tell me what I can and can't do."

"I hear you," he assured her. "I'm not trying to tell you what to do. I'm only making suggestions."

Cassie stood there, the pile of shirts clutched to her chest. "I understand," she said at last. "I don't mean to sound ungrateful. It's a generous offer, but I don't think you have any idea what it's like to live with two young girls underfoot."

"You are absolutely right," he admitted with a grin. "But my gut is telling me to stay with you. Close to you. And I'm willing to deal with a few days of chaos if it means we all sleep better at night." He paused. "Trust me, Winnie isn't going to let anybody near my place without everybody knowing it."

"Winnie the superdog," she said fondly.

"I told her about the cape, and she's looking forward to it." Brady shoved his hands into his pockets and rolled onto his heels. "She's as brave a beast as there ever was. At least until a thunderstorm comes rolling through."

"The girls don't like them either," Cassie told him. "Maybe they could all huddle together and I'd get to sleep solo for once."

Brady didn't allow himself to dwell too long on the image of Cassie Whitaker sprawled across the double bed in his spare room. He gave a businesslike nod, pulled his hands from his pockets and stepped out of her bedroom. "I'm going to make a call and let you finish packing. In the meantime, I'll try to figure out how we're going to fit two girls and one bed hog of a Labrador on the foldout futon in the third bedroom."

"Trust me, they'll find a way," Cassie called after him.

He gathered the backpacks she'd left in the hall, but lingered near the master bedroom as he called the station to report the break-in. He needed to be sure she didn't try to sneak a peek at the lipstick-scrawled threat on the bathroom mirror. Minutes later, he found Cassie shoving handfuls of what he could only assume were her undergarments into a duffel with a Blaze's River Tours and Rafting logo emblazoned on it.

She saw him watching and her cheeks stained a faint pink. "I'll need a new toothbrush and deodorant and stuff," she informed him.

"We can handle a run to the Stop & Shop," he assured her. "We'll also need to get some food you and the girls like to eat. I'm not much of a cook, so my meals at home mainly consist of breakfast cereal, microwave dinners and the occasional steak I can throw on the grill."

Cassie's face brightened. "I can cook. I love to cook." She zipped the duffel bag, shouldered it and then gave a decisive nod. "The girls and I will cook for you while we're there."

Brady grinned. "Sounds like a deal." He scratched his neck. "I guess I should apologize ahead of time. I can't really remember what condition I left my place in." When she gave him an amused glance, he shrugged and avoided her gaze. "Mainly I've been working on framing out the new house, but then..." He trailed off, not wanting to make her feel guilty for being the reason he hadn't been home in days.

"But then Keith Norton stole my daughters and you did everything humanly possible to get them home to me safe and sound," she said tartly. Blowing her hair away with a huff, she straightened and looked him dead in the eyes. "Brady Nichols, you never have to apologize to me for anything. Ever."

He grinned at her. "Be careful about making blanket statements to a guy. We remember those."

She snorted. "Probably the only things you ever remember a woman saying."

"Hey, now—"

"I'm only teasing." She pulled the bag from the end of the bed, cast a glance at the door to the adjoining bath, then straightened her shoulders. "You didn't have to worry about me sneaking a peek. If there's anything the last ten years has taught me, it's to not take the things men say when they're in the midst of a tantrum to heart."

"I understand." He ducked his head, slightly abashed by being so transparent. "Sorry."

"Again, no apologies needed. And you certainly don't have to worry about questionable housekeeping. The girls and I will pitch in. We'll also be helping to make a mess of it, so you'll see, everything will even out in the end."

The hopeful look on her face unlocked something inside of him. "I'm looking forward to it. Winnie is great, but not much for conversation."

"Okay, well, gird your ears. You're going to have plenty of chatter coming at you." She abandoned the bag and walked over to the dresser and picked up a small blown-glass figurine of a ballerina. "I bought this for my nana at the mall in Boise one year when I was about Brook's age."

"Did she like ballet?"

Cassie shook her head. "Not particularly. And I didn't dance. It was one of those kid gifts you buy your grandma because you have no clue what old people like. My parents gave me money to buy Christmas gifts, and I picked out the thing I thought was prettiest."

"She kept it."

"Of course. She was my nana." She glanced over at the closed bathroom door and rolled her shoulders, "And now I've brought this ugliness into her house."

He jerked with surprise when she pivoted and hurled the delicate figurine at the closed bathroom door. It shattered into thousands of tiny pieces which embedded themselves into the carpet. Cassie watched the shards settle there. "I guess it's too much to hope he'll come around barefoot."

"Probably a long shot," Brady agreed gruffly. "Feel any better?"

"It didn't hurt." Striding to the bed, she looped the strap on the duffel over her shoulder. "Okay," she said briskly. "I have everything I need from here, and you've got yourself a passel of houseguests invading your space." She cast one last glance at the closed bathroom door, then gave a visible shudder. "Let's get out of here."

"I called in and told Jenny to tell the technicians to be subtle about approaching the house," he said, following her down the hall. "They can enter through the rear door. We'll leave it open. It's possible he'll show up again. We'll make sure someone is keeping an eye on the place. Any neighbors we should inform?"

Cassie shook her head. "Only Mrs. Garbowski next door. I don't want to worry her. She's ninety-two and watches too much true crime on television."

"Gotcha."

She huffed a breath. "I doubt he returns. Keith may be a jerk, but he's a smart jerk."

"Okay then."

She paused in the living room and took one last look around, her expression mournful. "I used to visit every summer. I would stay with my grandparents for weeks and basically run wild." She slid him a sidelong glance. "They were—are—some of my best memories. But this house has felt strange without my grandparents in it, and now…" She swallowed hard, and Brady clutched the straps of the two backpacks he held tighter, hating to see her distress. "I guess I'll worry about where to go next later," she concluded.

Moved by her emotion, Brady took a step closer. "He can't steal your memories. This is still your grandparents' house, and soon it will feel like a safe place again," he assured her. "Your girls will grow up here. Maybe not running wild," he added with a pointed look. "But kids are resilient. Eventually, they will accumulate as many happy memories as you have of the place, and it will balance out the bad."

"I hope so," she said, a wistful note in her tone.

He gestured to the door. "This is a good town, Cassie. It's full of good memories for you and has plenty of adventures in store for the girls. I promise you we're gonna do everything we can to help make it feel safe again."

She put her hand on his arm. He felt the now-familiar jolt of attraction zing through him but quickly squelched it. He'd invited this formidable, yet still vulnerable, woman to bring her children to his house and stay. He wasn't about to do anything to make her feel uncomfortable there.

"Thank you," she said in a whisper. "You always seem to say exactly what I need to hear."

He ducked his head, pleased but embarrassed by the compliment. "I hope so."

She gave his arm a gentle squeeze, and it was all he could do to keep from jumping straight out of his skin. "We haven't known each other long, and certainly not under the best of circumstances, but I consider you a friend, Brady. I trust you. I trust you with my life, and more importantly, with my girls."

He blinked, wondering as he stared down into those wide hazel eyes if he'd been firmly and permanently placed into the friend zone. He hoped not, but he knew she couldn't be thinking about becoming anything more than friends. For now, he was grateful for her candor.

"Thank you. And I feel the same way about you." Recognizing he couldn't feel exactly the same because he wasn't entrusting her with his life or children, he gave a self-conscious scoff of a laugh, then gently tugged his arm from her grasp, unable to withstand the electricity pulsing through his veins one second longer. "I mean, I consider you a friend. I'm glad we're friends."

Cassie gazed at him watchfully for a beat longer, then gave him what had to be her first genuine smile since they'd arrived. "Okay then, friend. Let's go tell the girls they're going to have a slumber party with Winnie."

She glanced over her shoulder as they headed for the kitchen door. "Do you happen to keep any noise-canceling headphones handy? If not, we'd better buy some earplugs when we stop at the store, because when we tell them, you will be subjected to squealing guaranteed to hit decibel levels you'll wish only Winnie could hear."

Chapter Seventeen

Brady Nichols's place wasn't anything like what Cassie had envisioned. Not that she'd spent hours picturing his home, but based on what she knew of him—a divorced guy in his late thirties, living alone with his dog—she hadn't expected his place to be so…clean. The layout was pretty standard. A living room with a single shotgun hallway leading to three bedrooms and a full bath. A good-sized eat-in kitchen had a window above the sink and a door that led to a deck. Through the window, she could see the skeleton of the home he was building for his future.

His warnings about the state of the place were unnecessary. It seemed comfortable, if a bit dated. She couldn't imagine a guy Brady's age picking out some of the furniture. And other than a few dishes soaking in a sink of long-cooled water and a fine layer of dust in the living room, the place was spotless.

Of course, with her girls there, it wouldn't stay neat for long. She bit her lip, feeling torn about invading this man's world. He had no clue what he was in for.

Brady and Winnie led her daughters into a bedroom with a large futon sofa and a home office setup complete with a laptop sitting open on top of the wood-and-glass desk.

"Whoa, we get to stay here?" Jilly asked, plopping down on the sofa and giving a couple of experimental bounces.

"You do. It folds down into a bed," Brady explained, spotting Brook's dubious glance.

Cassie oh-so-casually moved to the desk, closed the laptop and stooped to disconnect the power cord. Brady shot her a quizzical look, and she shrugged as she straightened, the laptop clutched to her chest like a shield. "Trust me, you'll thank me later."

"Is that a computer?" Brook asked, right on cue. "I wanna use it!"

Cassie shook her head, cutting off any response Brady might have. These were her daughters and she would set the rules for them. "This is not our computer. Therefore, no, you cannot use it without asking for Brady's permission." She handed it over to the man in question. "My recommendation is that you do not grant permission unless you like having crumbs in your keyboard and a smudged-up screen."

Brady nodded solemnly, then his face broke into a wide grin. "I actually don't mind either of those things. But I do think maybe it would be better if you used it only when your mom or I can be around to oversee things. Sound like a deal?"

Brook's response was subdued, but she bobbed her head empathically. "Yes, sir," she replied.

"You can call me Brady," he told her.

Her grin flashed to full wattage, and Cassie had to blink away tears. Brook was always so serious. Her smiles felt like a gift on the best of days, and now mere hours after suffering one of the worst days in her young life, she was gracing Brady with one of the brightest smiles Cassie had ever witnessed from her eldest daughter.

"I can?" Brook asked, looking pleased by being invited onto such grown-up footing. She glanced hopefully at Cassie, waiting for parental consent.

After all they'd been through together, and the close proximity they would be in for at least a day or two, asking them to call him Officer Nichols seemed excessive. "If he says it's okay, it's okay with me."

"Computers are stupid," Jilly announced. She promptly flopped down onto the floor and sat cross legged, extending her arms open wide. "Dogs are so much better. Can I play with Winnie?"

"Again, Winnie is not ours," Cassie was quick to interject. "She's also a working—"

But the yellow Lab interrupted her lecture by pushing her way through their legs and sitting down directly in front of her younger daughter. The two eyed each other hopefully, then Jilly wrapped her skinny arms around the dog's neck in an exuberant hug.

"Not too tight now," Cassie warned automatically.

"Thank you," Jilly whispered into Winnie's fur. "Thank you for finding us."

Cassie's heart clenched. They'd been hanging out with the dogs at the station for hours, but now Jilly's narrow shoulders shook with tears as she hugged Winnie. Cassie's knees gave out and she knelt beside her, rubbing her narrow back.

"She's the bestest dog in the world," Jilly pronounced.

Cassie couldn't argue the sentiment. "Winnie is definitely our heroine," she said in an emotion-choked whisper. She glanced at Brady and found his expression wistful. Maybe even affectionate.

He cleared his throat. "Maybe while you girls stay with us, you'll help me make sure Winnie gets her dinner on time and her water bowl is clean?"

Jilly stared at him, hero worship written all over her face. "Oh yes," she exclaimed, nodding almost as enthusiastically as her sister had. "We'll help any way we can, won't we, Brookie?" she asked, turning to her big sister for confirmation.

Brook reached out to pat Winnie's head and stroke the dog's soft ears. "Yeah, sure. We love Winnie."

"When Momma says we can get a dog, I want to get one like Winnie," Jilly announced.

Brady chuckled. "Live with her a few days and you might want to look around a bit more. Labradors are great, but they take a lot of training," Brady said in a warning tone. "They're good pets, but they can get kind of lazy if you don't work with them a lot."

"Oh, we'll work with her," Brook said eagerly. "We'll need someone to show us what to do."

"Lucky for you, Winnie is a bit of a show-off," he said, his tone warm with affection.

"Okay, we need to get settled in and give Brady some space," Cassie insisted. "We went by the store on our way to get you guys. We're having tacos tonight."

The announcement was met with a chorus of "Yay!" which Winnie joined in on with a bark.

Brady grinned. "Tacos are a yay from me too."

Satisfied she made the right call, Cassie stood and moved closer to Brady's side. "I suggest you remove anything else from this room you might not want destroyed," she spoke in hushed tones. "They're curious girls and they tend to have fairly few boundaries."

Brady's grin grew wider. "I don't mind. Winnie and I are gonna enjoy having some company, I think." He glanced to where his dog had collapsed in front of the girls, allowing them to rub her belly and scratch behind her ears. The Labrador's pink tongue lolled out the side of her mouth, but her gaze still traveled to Brady as though she were checking to see if accepting their adoration was all right.

He laughed and said firmly, "Winnie, stay."

Cassie saw the tension literally melt away from the dog's prone posture. She pressed her head against Brook's knee and rolled over, her paws stretched in ecstasy as the girls continued their exuberant rubdown.

Ducking her head, she walked down the short hall toward the kitchen. Being in such close proximity to Brady Nichols was both wonderful and disconcerting. Wonderful because the man was a comfort. Disconcerting because he was a man, and hadn't she learned enough lessons where men were concerned?

"I'll get the groceries unpacked," she said, hoping to put enough distance between them to get her thoughts in order again.

But to her consternation, Brady followed. "I'll show you where everything is."

As she plunged her hand into one of the many bags

they had carried in from her van, she glanced over her shoulder, taking in the decent-sized kitchen and eating area. "I really didn't expect this place to be so spacious. It's nice. I was worried we'd be on top of you." The second the words were out of her mouth, her cheeks heated. The last thing she needed to do was start tossing innuendo around. She hoped Brady didn't take her comments out of context.

Thankfully, he seemed oblivious. She watched as he stowed packages of ground beef, chicken, and bags of frozen chicken nuggets into what appeared to be a freezer desperately in need of defrosting.

"Are you kidding me? My mouth is already watering at the thought of tacos." He waited until she looked over at him, then gestured to the boxes of frozen entrées in the iced-over freezer. "I'm not much of a cook."

"We'll be happy to earn our keep," she replied. "I'm no gourmet, but I've managed to keep those two alive for a few years. Maybe I can show you a thing or two, get you out of the frozen-entrée rut."

He chuckled and let the freezer door swing shut. "You can try, but I spend most of my off-hours working on the house. It's easier to nuke something than spend time in the kitchen preparing a meal for one." He waved a hand toward the window above the sink, and Cassie moved closer to take a better look at the large wood-framed structure they glimpsed as they pulled to the double-wide.

"I can't believe you're building a house. Amazing," she said as she let her gaze travel over the size of the foundation he'd laid out for a structure. It was much larger than the mobile home he lived in currently. "It looks like it's going to be pretty big."

He pointed to some of the exterior walls he and his friends erected. "Almost twice the square footage of what I have here. More than I need, but I didn't want to build something I'd have to add on to in order to make it marketable if I ever wanted to sell."

"Sell?" she asked, surprised by the notion. The house wasn't even built yet and he was already thinking ahead about putting it on the market?

Brady shook his head. "I have no plans to move anytime soon, but I figured if I was going to build a house, I was going to build one that would appeal to someone other than me."

"Wow." The thought of him casting his mind so far into the future was boggling to her. She'd been living day to day, week to week and month to month for so long, she couldn't imagine thinking beyond those markers. Brady was planning for a future ten, twenty or even thirty years out.

Cassie moved away from the window and focused on the array of shopping bags. "Smart thinking," she said as she pulled a box of crunchy taco shells from one of the bags. She shook her head. "I have no earthly idea where I'll be a month from now, much less years into the future."

"You don't plan to stay in Jasper?" he asked as he unpacked the next bag.

"I had hoped to," she confessed. It came out huskier than she'd intended. She cleared her throat, shook her head, then shot him a shaky smile. "I'd hoped this town would be the refuge for the girls it had been for me when I was young, but now… I don't know. Will the girls ever be able to move past this? Will I?"

Brady stopped and faced her head-on. "You will."

Chapter Eighteen

She was saved from needing to reply by the ringing of his cell. Brady's brows knit as he accepted the call and pressed the phone to his ear. He walked out the kitchen door for more privacy, and Cassie tried to ignore the twist in her gut. She couldn't simply assume every call he received was connected to her circumstances, nor did he owe her any insight into his personal life.

But she would be lying to herself if she didn't admit she was curious. As she finished putting the groceries away, she thought over the conversations they'd had, parsing them for any details she could winnow out. No, she wasn't mistaken. He hadn't mentioned anyone special in his life. Nor had he alluded to any desire to have someone. Sure, he might be building a big house out here on this pretty piece of property, but it didn't mean he envisioned a family to fill it. In fact, he'd spoken pretty plainly about his thoughts concerning re-sale value.

The certainty in his tone when he said she'd be able to move past their current predicament was heartening. She didn't know him well, but her gut said Brady was a straight shooter. He wouldn't blow hot air at her. If he thought she and her girls could get past Keith Norton's invasion in their lives, then he truly believed it.

She pulled out the brownie mix and went on the hunt for a mixing bowl. In a lower cabinet she found a large ceramic bowl with flowers printed around the outside and a chip in the lip. She placed it on the floor at her feet, and scanned the assortment of battered old pots and pans. When she heard his heavy footsteps she asked, "I don't suppose you have a cake pan, do you?"

Brady shook his head, but then indicated the disposable aluminum roasting pan he'd tossed into the cart at the store. "No, but I saw the brownie mix and grabbed one of these," he said, a hopeful gleam in his eyes.

One corner of her mouth curved as she eyed the deep roasting pan. "Ah, I see. Unfortunately, I would've had to purchase two boxes of mix to make a pan that big work."

"Really?" Brady asked in a tone so crestfallen, she was tempted to drive to the market to buy a second box of mix.

"Never mind. I can buy a smaller pan and we can bake them tomorrow."

Frowning, he jerked his head to the side, signaling for her to step out of the way. She did, and he dropped to his knees in the spot she'd vacated. "I have to have something that'll work."

Determination furrowed his brow. Apparently, Brady wanted those brownies. The clatter and scrape of pots and pans being moved and rearranged in an increasing crescendo of desperation made her want to laugh out loud. She bit her lip instead. Something told her Brady

Nichols would go running to the store again rather than ditch the idea of brownies.

"Hey, will this work?" he asked, his voice sounding oddly hollow from the inside of the cabinet. A second later, he pulled out a battered pie plate.

Unwilling to disappoint him, she took the pan he held aloft like a trophy. "Yes. I think I can make it work."

"Excellent," he hissed, sitting on his heels. "Tacos and brownies. My heart might not be able to handle any more excitement tonight."

His words were light, but there was something in his grim eyes that set alarm bells ringing in her head. "What? What is it?"

"Huh?" He froze for a split second, then placed the bowl she'd unearthed onto the counter with the pie pan inside it.

"Something's bothering you," she insisted.

He pressed his palms to his thighs, then lurched to his feet with a grunt of exertion. "It's, uh—" He rubbed his neck, clearly conflicted.

Cassie was coming to recognize the nervous gesture and respected it. She took a step closer to him. "If it's personal, you can tell me to butt out, but if it's something to do with the case, I need to be in the loop."

He raised dark eyebrows, pinning her with an assessing stare. "At this point, I'm not sure if it's anything."

"If it has anything to do with my daughters, then it's something."

"It's not directly about the girls," he said, but his gaze slid away from hers.

Evasion was not his strong suit. It was one of the things she liked most about Brady Nichols. He couldn't lie well, even if he wanted to. "Okay. If you want to play semantics, I can too. If whatever it is concerns anything to do with Keith Norton, then I have to be informed," she amended. "I'm the one who knows him."

Brady heaved a sigh. "I don't want to say anything because it could be absolutely nothing," he hedged.

"Brady…" she said in the same tone she used with the girls when they were trying to get around her.

"There's an old, abandoned lumberyard. We patrol it fairly regularly because there was some trouble out there not too long ago. That was Jason Wright calling. He's the young guy who got engaged the night of the, uh, party at the DCA."

"The night Keith Norton abducted my children," she corrected, each word hard as a rock.

"Yes." Brady ran his hand over his hair, then gave his neck a squeeze. "Jason says he's spotted some evidence someone may have been in the lumberyard recently."

She opened her mouth, but before she could get a word out, he waved his hands to stop her. "We have absolutely no proof or reason to believe it might have been Keith Norton in particular. Lots of people pass through these parts. People moving from one spot to another. People trying to get away from civilization."

"But it could have been Keith," she said in a rush, determined to wedge in the words.

Brady inclined his head in acknowledgment. "Jason and one of our other officers, Ava Callan, are checking the place more carefully. So far, it's some litter left behind, but if they find anything hinting it may be Norton, they'll be sure to give me a heads-up right away."

Cassie fixed him with her sternest mom glare. "And you'll give me one," she stated flatly.

Brady stared at her, his jaw tensing until the tiny muscle in the corner jumped beneath his beard. "If there's anything you need to be aware of, I'll be sure to tell you," he promised.

Cassie heaved a sigh and turned to the counter, where she pried open the box of brownie mix. Pulling the chipped mixing bowl closer to her, she said, "I guess that'll have to be good enough. For now." The two of them held each other's gaze, both wordlessly trying to convey their immovable will.

In the end, Cassie couldn't have said which one of them would have won if Jilly hadn't interrupted. "Mama, can Winnie and I help you make the brownies?"

Chapter Nineteen

Brady rose early the next morning, put on his uniform and had Winnie in her harness before he realized he would be leaving Cassie and the girls in his house unattended. He stood in the front entry listening to their morning chatter bubble out of the kitchen, completely torn about what to do.

A part of him really wanted to be on the job. A bigger part of him needed to be involved in the search for Keith Norton. Jason and Ava hadn't been able to find anything more than scattered evidence of someone being in the abandoned lumberyard, but nothing tying the detritus left behind directly to Norton.

Brady wasn't surprised. The man was smart. He'd cover his tracks. Leaving the truck at the end of the fire lane had been a lucky stroke for them, and they'd bungled it. They should have impounded the vehicle immediately. But the truck itself wasn't his main concern. The man had managed to thread the needle on their surveillance once. His adversary seemed to be one step ahead of them. It made Brady uneasy.

His gut told him Norton was still in the area. The girls hadn't been physically harmed. The message on the mirror made it clear Cassie was the one Norton was after. Having spent a scant couple of days in the woman's company, Brady could understand how a man could get so sucked into her orbit. It would be hard for any guy to watch a woman so strikingly self-possessed walk away. Something about her unapologetic confidence made a man want to strive to be better. To be needed. But unlike Norton's kind, Brady ached to be wanted as much as he was needed.

He wouldn't mind one bit if a woman like Cassie decided he was the one for her. She was beautiful, but easy and natural. He liked the way they interacted. Liked how they could talk openly and honestly, but could also sit comfortably in silence. Even when her tension and worry for her daughters had to have been crushing her.

The fact that she was a mother didn't lessen her attractiveness but rather enhanced it. Seeing the way she faced life head-on, but still remained soft enough to give her girls everything they needed, was extremely appealing.

Brady knew he was far too susceptible to the lure of her, so his first thought upon waking had been to get out of there. He needed to give himself some space to breathe and to get his thoughts in order. If she didn't plan to stay in Jasper, there was no point in trying to start anything.

He wanted to put down roots. The structure behind the trailer was proof of permanence. He wanted the family he'd been denied in his marriage. He'd always wanted a family. Was building a house large enough to accommodate one. He wanted the quieter small-town upbringing for his kids. Basically, he'd wanted everything his ex hadn't. He'd picked this place, this life, on purpose. Jasper was where Cassie came when she needed refuge. He hoped it wasn't a convenient pit stop on the way to something different. He planned to be one of the old goats hanging around the town square watching the passersby and yammering a constant stream of commentary.

His were simple life goals, but they made him happy thinking about them. Usually. But thinking about them both with and without Cassie Whitaker in the picture stirred some emotional turmoil.

Stroking Winnie's head, he looked down and gave the dog a pat. "I think we could use some distance today, don't you, girl?"

She must have tuned in to his plan using her I'm-a-mom supersensory hearing, because Cassie appeared in the kitchen doorway. "Heading to work?"

Though she phrased it as a question, the observation came out sounding more like a statement. "Yeah, I have a shift this morning and I want to review what's going on with the investigation. Will you be all right here by yourselves?"

Cassie's chin lifted an inch. "Of course, we will." Then she seemed to catch the defensiveness in her tone, and her expression softened. "You haven't had breakfast," she pointed out. "Hang on a minute."

He didn't usually eat breakfast, but she disappeared into the kitchen without giving him a chance to say so. A minute later, she reappeared cradling a napkin-wrapped pancake in her hand.

He glanced down to see she had layered scrambled egg with two strips of bacon, then drizzled maple syrup onto it and curled the edges upward. She presented it to him with a flourish. Breakfast eater or not, Brady's mouth watered.

"I figured since you were such a fan of last night's tacos, you wouldn't mind a sort of twist on them," she said, looking eager to please.

He took the offering from her. "No, ma'am. This looks fantastic."

Cassie beamed down at Winnie. "I have something for you too," she assured the dog as she conjured one of the small crunchy bones Brady kept in a jar on the counter as part of Winnie's training reward system.

He didn't have the heart to tell Cassie he didn't give his dog treats on a just-because basis. Winnie accepted the offering gingerly, then glanced at him for permission. Unable to deny her, he nodded and Winnie chomped down on the bone with such glee, they both chuckled at the dog.

"Good girl," he said automatically.

Cassie moved a step away, then put her hands in the pockets of her shorts. "I'm sorry, I probably should have asked first, but she is a good girl, and she deserves all the treats in the world as far as I'm concerned."

"I get you, but yeah. I try to save those for training and working situations."

Her eyes flared with rebellion. "Well, she did keep watch over the girls all night."

"She did," Brady concurred, letting her off the hook. He patted his pockets, checked the utility belt to be sure he'd clipped his phone in with the rest of his equipment, then jangled his car keys. "You have my number. You'll text if anything at all bothers you." He stated the last as fact, not a request, his gaze fixed on her in an unwavering stare he hoped commanded acquiescence.

To his relief, Cassie didn't make a fuss. "Absolutely."

"Good. And it goes both ways," he assured her. "I'll text you if I find out any new information."

"I would appreciate being kept in the loop."

Brady lifted the makeshift breakfast taco in salute, then turned toward the front door. "You girls have a good day. Make yourselves at home, and don't worry about making a mess of the place." He pointed to the skeletal structure behind the double-wide. "This is temporary."

Cassie grinned at him. "Maybe this evening you'll give us a tour of the site? I'd love to see what you have planned for the house."

Her genuine interest sent a wave of warmth through him. No, his instincts were right. He needed to put distance between himself and this entrancingly earnest woman. Through sheer force of will, he tamped down the pride aching to burst out of him.

"I'd be glad to," he replied casually.

"Have a good day," she called after him.

The words were so simple. Her wish for him such an everyday sort of sentiment it made his chest tighten. He wanted to hear them each time he left for work. Stepping out onto the small porch with Winnie hot on his heels, he answered gruffly, "You too." With his gaze fixed on his vehicle, he called over his shoulder, "And lock the doors behind me."

"Oh, don't you worry, I will," Cassie assured him.

At the foot of the steps, he paused to listen until he heard the click of the locks on the front door. Then, and only then, did he allow himself to raise the pancake-wrapped breakfast taco to his mouth and take a large bite. The explosion of sweet and salty under his tongue nearly sent his brain into overload.

How would he ever be able to stomach microwave meals again?

A bit of a scrambled egg fell to the ground, and Winnie stared down at it, prepared to lunge if only he'd give the go-ahead. Brady sighed contentedly as he chewed. "Okay, fine. Eat," he commanded.

The dog wolfed down the bit of egg and gazed at him with hopeful amber eyes.

Brady shook his head, then pointed toward the truck. "Not gonna happen. And don't get used to extra cookies either," he warned her. "You're the hero of the hour so you're getting a few bonus treats, but we'll be on austerity measures from here on out," he said, trying for a stern tone.

Winnie's pink tongue lolled out the side of her mouth as she trotted alongside him, glancing at the food hopefully. He walked slowly, taking huge, greedy bites. Somehow he managed to fold the pancake just right and the syrup seemed to be holding things together as he snarfed the last couple of bites.

Winnie looked crestfallen. He chuckled as he opened the door and gestured for her to hop in. But she was a crafty dog. She gave his syrup-sticky fingers a few surreptitious licks while he secured her harness.

"We're both going to gain ten pounds in the next week. And what kind of search team would that make us?" he asked his partner. "We'll be crashing through those woods like a bowling ball."

Winnie simply panted in response. She had absolutely no problem with this possibility.

Chuckling to himself, he closed the passenger door, wiped his hands on the now sticky napkin Cassie had wrapped around the taco, then slid into the driver's seat.

Thankfully he had some antibacterial gel in the console to remove the rest of the syrupy residue. Once they were all set, he started the truck and cranked the wheel. The clearing he'd made in front of the trailer was wide, even if the lane he'd cut for access to the property wasn't. Sometimes his friends would help on weekends. Gradually, they'd carved out ample parking. But he never expected to be maneuvering around a minivan so soon.

Chapter Twenty

On the drive into town, he forced himself to think of all the next steps he had upcoming with the house rather than the attractive woman and two vulnerable children he'd left alone in his double-wide, miles from the nearest neighbor.

As he drove past the sign marking the Jasper city limits, Brady kept his eyes peeled for anyone who didn't look like they belonged. Familiarity was one of the perks of a small town. Even with the tourists who flocked to the Salmon River, it was easy to tell they were there with a purpose.

Though he hadn't lived in Jasper long, he knew many of the town's residents well enough to exchange a wave. Plus, gossip was a major form of currency around these parts, so if Norton had shown his face at any of the local establishments, there was a good chance he'd hear about it. There was no doubt in his mind nearly everyone was aware of the kidnapping and that the perpetrator hadn't been caught. Jasper would be on high alert.

At the station, he parked his truck next to Dillon's, collected his partner and headed for the front door. He tried to pretend he was reporting for duty like he would on any other day. But this was not a normal day. He felt tense and jittery. Winnie was attentive. And when they stepped into the station, he could feel the kinetic energy coursing through the place.

"The chief would like to see you," Teresa said in a low tone.

Brady suppressed a groan. "Sure. Of course."

It stood to reason the big boss would want a full report on everything Brady knew at this point, but he had to assume Captain Rutledge would be sitting in on the meeting. As the chief's heir apparent, Arthur Rutledge was wheedling his way into more and more top-level conversations within the department. And having Rutledge in his business was almost as annoying as the questions Brady was sure the man would ask.

He raised his hand in greeting to his fellow officers as he and Winnie wended their way through the warren of desks. He caught Dillon's eye and angled his head in the direction of the chief's office. His friend grimaced for him. Stopping by his desk, he deposited his keys and wallet in the center drawer, then removed Winnie's lead. The dog curled on the bed beside his desk, her eyes fixed on him as she settled in.

"Good girl. Stay."

Winnie rested her chin on her front paws and let her eyelids droop. After all, Labradors loved an early-morning nap. Heck, they loved anytime naps, Brady thought, chuckling to himself as he made his way to the chief's office. It was a marvel his partner got anything accomplished at all, given her affinity for a good snooze. Dogs were amazing creatures.

He paused outside the office door, then rapped twice with his knuckles.

At the bellowed "Come in!" he reached for the handle.

Brady opened the door and found Rutledge lounging in one of the chairs across from Chief Walters's desk. He tamped down a flare of annoyance and gave each man a cordial nod. "Good morning."

Rutledge did nothing but nod, but the chief gave him an encouraging smile. "Morning, Nichols. I trust you had an uneventful night?"

Brady thought about the pleasant evening he'd spent with Cassie, Brook and Jilly. The girls had been quiet at first, but with Winnie nearby, Jilly was quick to bounce back. However, both girls stayed close to their mother, Brady had noted. Even Brook. Though, as the elder, she held herself aloof. She was nine and not a baby anymore, she'd reminded him, offended by his offer to pour her a glass of juice.

But yeah, it had been a good night. An uneventful night, thank goodness. The tacos had been delicious, and the brownies hit the spot even if they were thick and unevenly baked from being prepared in a pie plate. He didn't mind. The fudgier the better as far as he was concerned. All in all, the evening passed in a haze of exhausted camaraderie. Somehow the four of them had formed a unit. Five of them, really, because Winnie was more a part of the group than he was, he suspected.

"Everything went well. The girls seem to be settling in, and I think it helped to have Winnie nearby. They like the dog, and she can be pretty comforting when she wants to be."

"She's a service dog," Rutledge interjected briskly. "You shouldn't let them treat her like a family pet."

Brady's jaw tightened. There was no point in arguing the finer points of canine training with Arthur Rutledge. The man didn't see the value in the K-9 partnership they'd formed with the Daniels Canine Academy, and more than a few of the officers were concerned Rutledge would do away with the program altogether once he was in charge.

He inclined his head in acknowledgment, then turned his attention to the chief. "I've spoken to Ms. Whitaker about requesting some sessions with therapists who came to see the girls in the hospital. It would be great if they could speak to them again today, if possible. I think the more they talk about what happened, the better off they'll be."

Rutledge snorted softly but didn't say anything because the chief was already nodding emphatically. "Yes. It's important kids talk about things. Otherwise they bottle their emotions up."

Chief Walters steepled his fingers. "I put in a call to county services already, so you may want to make sure Ms. Whitaker is aware someone will be reaching out to her."

"Will do." He turned his attention to Rutledge. "Any new leads, Captain?"

Rutledge darted an encompassing gaze to Chief Walters, then returned his attention to Brady, who did his best not to bristle. The man supposedly had direct responsibility for this investigation, but he didn't seem to be ready to share whatever they'd been discussing with him.

When there was no answer forthcoming, he pushed with the information he had. "They didn't find anything conclusive at the old lumberyard, but there are some other spots around town Winnie and I could check out. Maybe the mill? I could ask around some at the local businesses to see if they've seen Norton. I think we should also alert the folks out at Blaze's. Some of their fishing cabins are pretty remote, and if they're not checking them daily, he could have used one of them as a squat."

Rutledge waved a hand. "Already on it with Blaze's and the other businesses. If you want to take the dog out to the lumberyard and the mill to have a sniff around, it couldn't hurt," he said, shifting his gaze to the chief, who nodded approvingly.

Rutledge might not have been a fan of the canine additions to their department, but he was no fool. He knew Chief Walters was the one who instigated the program, and he wasn't going to stomp on it in front of the man.

Brady opted to take him at his word. "Will do. Should I bring anyone with me, or—"

Rutledge shook his head. "No. We can't assign any additional resources to this until we have something concrete to investigate," he said, his tone a shade too brusque for Brady's liking. "The Feds are already involved. They have more to work with than we do."

Thankfully, the big guy stepped in. "As far as JPD is concerned, this is your case, Brady," he interjected. "If you find something where you think you need additional resources, we'll provide them. Until we have something that indicates the need for more manpower, we'd like you to take the lead on it."

Brady appreciated how Chief Walters's years of experience had shaved the edges off. His order was essentially the same as the one Rutledge had given, but was completely different in tone. "Yes, sir."

He turned to leave the office, but froze when Rutledge called after him. "Oh, and Nichols?"

Brady glanced over his shoulder. "Captain?" he responded, refusing the call the man *sir*. He hadn't earned his respect as of yet.

"We're willing to let this go on for a couple more days, but if there are no signs of Norton in the area, we will need to turn our attention to the usual matters again."

Brady's hand tightened on the doorknob. The urge to look at the chief to see if the older man approved this plan was strong, but Brady was also savvy. The future of his career would lie in Rutledge's hands one day. Openly defying or second-guessing the man's decisions would not play well. The captain was the kind of man who kept score.

"Understood," he replied tersely. "I'll go check out those locations and keep you briefed on my findings."

"And we appreciate what you're doing to keep Ms. Whitaker and her daughters feeling more secure. I hope having them as houseguests isn't putting you out too much," the chief added, eyes twinkling.

"No, sir. No trouble at all."

Brady pulled the door closed behind him, shut his eyes and let out a huge exhale. It bothered him that Rutledge riled him so much. Arthur was a good officer. He wasn't corrupt or self-serving. But the man's ambivalence toward the K-9 program, a program that had turned out to be life-changing for Brady, made him chafe. Rutledge's innate obnoxiousness made him an easy target for animosity among the officers who worked for him, though. Brady hated how easily the guy could push his buttons.

Keeping his gaze straight ahead, he walked through the maze of desks until he reached Dillon's. "So, I hear you've all been pulled off the Whitaker case."

His friend's gaze never wavered from Brady's. "Yeah. You know how it is." He shot a glance at Rutledge's empty office. "But, you know, keep us posted." Got it. Dillon wouldn't be working the case in any official capacity, but if Brady needed him, his buddy would be there.

Brady glanced over to where Cal Hoover watched them with a scowl on his face. "Yep, moving on to other things," Cal said gruffly. "Maybe we'll hand out some speeding tickets today."

Brady chuckled as he shook his head. "You guys have anything I can add to the file?" he asked, not liking the troubled look in Hoover's eyes.

Cal shook his head and shifted in his seat. "No. Nothing concrete. I've got a creepy feeling. He's been too quiet. No one has seen anything, and that's not normal around here."

Brady had the same itch between his shoulder blades. There was more happening than they knew about. Norton was going to make a move, and the suspicion sent shiver after shiver down Brady's spine. "Nobody is aware they're staying out at my place, are they?"

He shifted his gaze between the two men, but Dillon

broke first with a shrug. "Nobody *knows*," he said, emphasizing the word, "but, of course, some people know."

Brady wished the riddle didn't make sense to him, but he'd lived in Jasper long enough to both admire and disparage how well the grapevine worked. He also knew not everybody on the grapevine was good people. "Well, if you talk to one of those people, would you make sure they keep the information quiet. Norton could still be around. That was the whole point of them staying out at my place."

"We will be sure to remind them, but the people who may be clued in are people we can trust," Dylan assured him.

"Let's hope so," Brady said grimly. "In the meantime, any suggestions for where I might go kicking over some dead logs?" he asked both men.

Cal gave a shrug. "We've asked about everybody who's got a business here in the downtown area, and nada. The lumberyard was our first indication of anything possibly Norton related, but the search was inconclusive."

"Some people steer clear of the places cops go," Dillon said. "I think you should check out the places we *don't* frequent to ask a few questions."

Brady nodded his agreement. There were a few businesses outside the immediate vicinity of downtown Jasper. They weren't the places he and the other cops went to grab a beer after work or stopped in for lunch. Some were more attuned to the tourist trade Blaze's River Tours brought in, but there were also a couple of establishments where elements of society who didn't necessarily appreciate a police presence gathered. "Good call."

He raised a hand in farewell, then returned to his desk to collect Winnie. "I'll keep you updated," he called over his shoulder to no one in particular.

But it was Teresa who spoke as he snapped Winnie's lead onto the harness.

"Please do," she ordered, holding a key fob to one of the department's SUVs.

Winnie followed him toward the receptionist's desk at a trot. Teresa was always good for a scratch behind the ears. The older woman obliged the dog, then said, "Here," as she held out a plastic container filled with his favorite chocolate chip cookies. "Take these too. For energy."

Brady accepted the gift with a grin. "You're the best," he told her, pressing a hand over his heart.

"And don't you forget it," she said as he and Winnie pushed through the double doors.

"Never," Brady promised, then headed out to hunt for Keith Norton.

Chapter Twenty-One

He drove through the empty lots of the former JPG Lumber, his eyes peeled for any sign of activity, but failed to spot anything. He and Winnie stopped to search the area where Jason said he'd found the litter and other evidence of someone in residence, but the dog could not pick up any scent outside of the immediate area. Whoever had been there had driven in and driven out.

Determined to widen his circle, he drove out to the old mill. A few years ago, somebody had bought the property and tried to convert it into an ice cream parlor meant to attract tourists heading to and from the Salmon River. Apparently, business had not been as brisk as the owners had hoped because the ice cream parlor closed in the same season, and as far as he knew, no one had maintained the property. The second they jumped down from the SUV, Winnie had her nose pressed to the ground, but her ears remained flat against her head. Brady stood and surveyed the historic old place. There were plenty of places for someone to hide. They checked all the doors and windows, but nothing looked to be disturbed.

He gave Winnie plenty of lead to take him in any direction that caught her fancy. But while the dog found many scents of interest, none of them piqued her curiosity enough to warrant more than a cursory search of the perimeter.

At the car, he made sure to fill Winnie's portable water bowl to the brim, then chugged a bottle himself. The day was warm and the sun was high. Sweat dampened his uniform shirt, and he could feel droplets trickle down his temples. He ran the cool plastic bottle over his forehead. He exhaled loud and long, wiping away the mixture of sweat and condensation with his forearm. There were no signs of Norton here, and the longer he was away from home, the more uneasy he grew.

The property he purchased outside of town seemed idyllic with its wide-open pasture and the untamed woods he'd chosen as the backdrop for his newly built home. Now, all he could think was Cassie and the girls were too isolated out there. It was miles to even the Daniels place, his nearest neighbor. Setting his bottle on the roof of the SUV, he and Winnie moved into the shade provided by the vehicle, and he pulled his phone from the clip on his belt and began to text.

Everything okay?

Brady hadn't realized he was holding his breath until the flashing ellipses appeared, signaling typing on the other end.

Depends. How do you feel about beef stroganoff?

His thumbs flew over the screen.

I feel strong approval for beef stroganoff. Is there anything I can get for you while I'm in town?

The three dots appeared, then disappeared, then they
appeared again.

I guess I'll use this roasting pan. We can have ice cream
for dessert.

Involuntarily, Brady turned to look at the abandoned
ice cream parlor. It hadn't been a bad idea. He would
have enjoyed taking Cassie and her girls out for an ice
cream cone after dinner.

He had to stop thinking about those sorts of things.
They weren't dating. She wasn't staying at his house
because she liked him and wanted to be with him. They
were together only because some guy had decided he
had the right to invade her life.

Turning his attention back to his phone, he began
typing again.

Ice cream sounds great. I'll text later to see if you need
anything else from the store.

Her reply appeared almost instantly.

I have a car.

His jaw clenched as he stared at her reply. Of course,
she did. He wasn't holding her captive at his place. But

surely she understood the need to keep a low profile around town. He looked down at the screen, and the dancing dots reappeared and a second message from Cassie came through.

Sorry. Knee-jerk reaction. It's better if we stay here and lay low for a couple of days.

Thumbs poised, Brady composed multiple answers in his head, but decided simpler was better.

Call if you need anything.

Then he reattached the phone to his utility belt, opened the door for Winnie to hop in and secured the dog in her harness. "Winnie, you can't let me go thinking we have something more to go home to, okay? I need you to keep me in check." The dog panted contentedly, and he stroked her head. "It's you and me, right, girl?"

Bending to collect her water bowl from the disintegrating gravel parking area, he murmured to himself, "I need to remember. It's just you and me."

Brady had decided early on to make the Shaker Peak Bar and Grill the last stop on his general search for Keith Norton. He'd been avoiding it. He'd gone out with the woman who tended the bar a couple of times not long after moving to Jasper, but nothing ever developed between them. Much to Alyssa's chagrin.

Situated midway between town and the access to the Salmon River, Shaker Peak attracted a good number of out-of-towners to go along with the day drinkers who parked themselves on the stools and whiled away their days in a bar.

He left the vehicle running to keep Winnie cool as he went inside. Hopefully, he'd be able to get in and out with no more than a few cursory questions and answers.

Alyssa rocked onto her heels and crossed her arms over her chest as she gave him a pretty effective stink eye. "Well, well, well. Look what the doggy dragged in," she said in a mocking tone. "How's your girlfriend? What was her name again? Wendy? Ginny?"

Brady approached the bar with no hitch in his stride. "Hello, Alyssa. You're looking well. Business good?"

Alyssa, who never wanted to take the high road, rolled her eyes. "Booming," she said, casting a glance at the three grizzled men parked at the other end of the bar. Brady took a look around and saw only a single table of young college-aged guys obviously fresh from a day on the river. Besides them, there were no other occupants.

"What can I do for you?"

Brady wasn't offended by her brusque manner. He appreciated her getting right down to brass tacks. Unclipping his phone, he found the picture of Keith Norton and held it out for her. "Have you seen this man?"

He watched her face carefully. He could see recognition kicked in. He also had a creeping feeling again as she averted her gaze and snatched a damp towel off the bar.

"Can't say as I remember," she replied.

"Alyssa," he said, gentling his tone. "Have you? It's important."

She clutched the damp towel as she crossed her arms

over her chest again, but she still wouldn't meet his eyes. Instead, she focused on the door behind him. Maybe she was expecting someone to save her from his interrogation.

No one did, and there was no way Brady was leaving without getting what she didn't want to tell him out of her.

"This have something to do with those girls everyone's goin' on about? The ones who were taken?" she demanded.

"This is the man who took them," he answered without equivocating. "Have you seen him?"

"I didn't hear anything about it until Mavis Clausen came in here at lunchtime whining about how her nerves were shot," she informed him. "I told her she didn't need to make excuses to me, but then she started spilling her guts about how some horrible man had snatched two kids right out from under the noses of nearly everyone in town." She scoffed. "Including most of our police department."

Brady refused to take the bait. "You *have* seen him," he said, his tone flat but insistent.

She glanced over at the trio of barflies. He wondered if she was looking for backup or escape. They were too engrossed in dissecting the baseball game airing on a muted television mounted above the bar. "Maybe I have. Not sure."

"You are too." Brady thrust the phone out until it was an inch from her nose. "When? What did he want?"

She batted his arm away. "Stop."

Brady lowered the phone, but leaned in. "What did you tell him?"

She shrugged, but then her shoulders crept toward her ears as she crossed her arms again, her fingertips biting into her bare biceps. "He came in last night looking for the blonde who works down at the diner every once in a while. Vera's niece. Said they were old… friends."

Brady ignored the emphasis she put on the last word, needing to keep his cool. "What did you tell him?"

"Nothing. I told him she sometimes worked at the diner. He asked where she stayed, and I told him I thought she was living in her granny's old place, but I doubted she was home."

Then at last she met his eyes. "I heard you two are staying together, so I told him he might be able to find her with her policeman boyfriend," she said, drawling the last two words.

Brady closed his eyes on a cringe. "Did you give him any names?"

She shook her head. "Why would I? If he's stupid enough to still hang around after I told him his lady friend is shacking up with a cop, then he doesn't have the sense God gave a goose."

Brady didn't see the point in pursuing the line of questioning anymore. Whatever damage had been done, he couldn't undo it, so he gave Alyssa his most stern cop stare and spoke in a flat tone. "Cassie Whitaker is not my girlfriend. She is a nice lady whose daughters were taken from her by a man who appears to be stalking her," he said, speaking slowly and succinctly. "I'm sure as a fellow woman you can understand how afraid she must be. But this man was bold enough to walk off with her girls in the middle of a party most of the town, and as you pointed out, most of the police force, was attending." He let those stark facts sink in for a beat, then added, "If he does show himself again, I would appreciate you giving somebody at the station—doesn't have to be me—a call."

With nothing left to say, Brady turned on his heel and strode toward the door. He needed to talk to the chief about sticking close to home for a couple days.

Chapter Twenty-Two

Cassie had to wait until the girls left the room to add the sour cream to the stroganoff. For some reason they were convinced it was gross, and if they saw her add it, they wouldn't eat it. All things considered, they'd had a pretty good day at Brady's place. She'd straightened here and there, and enlisted the girls' help in deciding what they could cook to fill their hero's freezer.

Jilly had voted for chicken noodle soup, her personal favorite, but Brook's sophisticated taste ran more to the lasagna end of the spectrum. After they'd inspected what she'd already procured from the store, Cassie texted a short list to Brady. He had replied to it with a terse Will do.

The brief response set her teeth on edge. A part of her thought the sight of lasagna noodles on the list might have stirred more excitement in the man, but maybe she overestimated the lure of her culinary skills. Now she was worried he wouldn't like her invading his space in such a way. The notion hadn't occurred to her until she discovered the mother lode of plastic leftover containers stored in the bottom cabinets. It appeared Brady Nichols was not above relying on the kindness of others when it came to scoring a home-cooked meal. And she didn't have to stretch her imagination to figure some of those meals were likely prepared by single women auditioning for the role of personal chef. The thought of other women feeding Brady made her irrationally irritated.

She'd placed the stroganoff in the oven to keep warm when the front door opened and Winnie barreled into the house. The big yellow dog made a beeline for her water bowl, sloppily lapping the liquid in great, greedy gulps, then gazed at Cassie. The dog seemed unperturbed. Maybe she came home to a strange woman in the kitchen every day. Cassie had no idea what Brady's lifestyle might be. For all she knew, he was a serial dater.

Thankfully, a chorus of squealed greetings rent the air, jarring her from her thoughts.

Winnie bounded off to the left to meet the girls halfway down the hall, and Cassie found Brady carrying bags of groceries into the house.

Instantly contrite, she rushed to relieve him of some of the burden. "I would have helped carry those in."

"No problem." He sniffed the air, then gave a gratifying groan of approval. "Man, this is probably something Winnie and I shouldn't get too used to. We've never come home to the house smelling so good."

"Oh." The compliment sent a warm flush to her cheeks and made her ears burn. "I'm glad it smells good. I thought you might like something nicer than tacos from a kit."

Brady placed the remaining bags on the counter and turned to her. "Are you kidding me? Those tacos were gourmet compared to the frozen burritos I usually nuke."

She laughed. "I'll add the stroganoff leftovers to your collection of frozen entrées. The girls and I were thinking we could help stock you with some better options." She cocked her head to the side. "What do you think?"

"I think, yes, please," he responded with gratifying swiftness.

"Jilly voted for chicken noodle soup, and Brook thought you might like lasagna, but we're open to making whatever you want," Cassie said as she slid her hands into the battered oven mitts she'd found in a drawer. "I didn't want to overstep, but we want to show our appreciation to you for letting us stay here."

"There's no need."

"I've seen the sad state of your freezer. There's great need."

Brady's expression settled into a grim line of concern she was growing far too familiar with. He shifted his weight, scratching the corner of his jaw. It was a good thing the man hadn't set his sights on being a professional poker player. His earnest expression practically telegraphed his every thought.

"What is it?" she demanded.

He shot her an exasperated look. "Either you're a mind reader, or I need to work on my acting skills."

"It's hard to raise kids without being able to read people's expressions. My girls are like tiny tornadoes. When it comes to reading a room, I've gotten pretty good at dialing in to the barometric pressure."

He chuckled. "I bet you have."

"What's bothering you, Brady?"

His head jerked and she realized she'd never called him by his first name. At least, not like that. Somehow, it sounded intimate, and possibly overfamiliar. The heat in her cheeks intensified, but she hid it by ducking to extract the pan from the oven. "You might as well tell me. I won't let you rest until you do."

"Is that how you get them to clean their rooms?"

She caught his wry tone as she straightened. Placing the stroganoff atop the stove, she turned to look him square in the eye. "It's how I get them to do anything. It's my mom superpower." And in saying so, she widened her stance and planted her fists on her hips, staring him down as she did with the girls. "I think this arrangement of ours is going to work better for all of us if we speak our minds."

She wanted to retract the words almost immediately. They had no "arrangement," and she couldn't actually speak her mind. Couldn't tell him she found him to be the most attractive man she'd met in…forever. Not only because he was a winner in the looks department, but also in terms of personality and integrity. She'd stupidly dumped all of her dirty laundry about the ugliness of her previous relationships on him. Why would a man like Brady want to take on a woman with as much baggage as she was hauling around?

"You're right." He drew a deep breath and bent his head to the side to stretch his neck in a way she was coming to recognize as a prelude to bad news. "Keith Norton is still around town. I don't have any evidence other than a sighting as of yesterday, but I'm pretty sure he hasn't given up."

"He wouldn't," she stated flatly. "Why would he? He's already put too much on the line. He won't stop until he gets what he wants."

"He wants you," Brady stated flatly.

Cassie snorted. "No, he thinks he wants me because I didn't want him. He doesn't really want me. He wants to win," she said grimly.

"Either way, he's got you marked as his prize."

Cocking her own head to mirror the tilt of his, she studied the man beside her. "I'm damn tired of men acting like they get to lay claim to me."

"No man has the right," he said without missing a beat.

"Exactly. You get it, but you're not like other men," she said with a scornful sneer.

But what she said was true. Brady was not like other men. He was calm and steady. He was her port in a storm, but he was also as easy to be around as the yellow dog he called his partner.

He gave her a skeptical glance, and she shrugged. "You aren't," she insisted. "It's what makes you a good cop. Makes you a good man. You have integrity and self-confidence most other men, at least those of my acquaintance, act like they have but rarely do."

He swallowed hard. "Thank you," he said gruffly.

"It's the truth. And the truth is always easy to share." She held his gaze for a beat too long, then forced herself to turn away, busying her hands at the sink. "Go on and change. Vera dropped off some green beans left over from lunch at the diner. I called her because I couldn't remember the last time the girls ate something green, and I wasn't thinking too clearly when we went to the grocery store. Anyway, after dinner, the girls and I would like a tour of your house, if you don't mind."

He pushed away from the counter, looking pleased. "You're really interested in my house?"

She bobbed her head enthusiastically. "We stood on the deck trying to guess what rooms would be where when it's finished, but it's hard with no actual walls." Reaching for the skillet she'd used to make the stroganoff sauce, she glanced over at him, eager to reassure him they had been careful not to overstep any boundaries. "Don't worry, I wouldn't let them go out there. I told them it's a construction site and there could be dangerous things around."

He blew out a breath and ran his hand through his hair as he turned to look out the kitchen window. "There is. Let me go out and pick up some tools and such. I'll give you the grand tour after we eat."

"Sounds like a plan," she said as she poured the sauce over the beef and noodles.

Dinner was boisterous. The four of them sat crammed together at the tiny round table in Brady's eat-in kitchen. Of course, the girls complained mightily when they saw the green beans she'd spooned onto their plates, but when Brady helped himself to a second spoonful there was a marked shift in attitude. He'd bought a loaf of crusty bread from the grocery store's bakery aisle, and they all ate thick hunks of it slathered with butter.

She sat back and for the first time in hours, let her shoulders slump. She liked how easy Brady was with her daughters. He didn't talk down to them like so many adults did with children. Which probably explained why her girls responded to him with such ease.

She'd been worried. No doubt they'd deal with some tough moments thanks to the trauma Keith Norton had put them through, but right here and right now, everything was good.

The bread was warm, soft and fragrant, the stream of chatter from her girls, a reassuring soundtrack for the meal. Brady laughed at one of Brook's comments, and she felt her lips twitch into a smile. She glanced over at Brady and found him watching her with an expression of mild concern.

With a quick shake of her head, she indicated there was nothing wrong. Picking up her fork, she granted herself permission to enjoy the comfort of both the food and the company.

Her girls were safe. Brady was here, and so was Winnie. All was well.

Chapter Twenty-Three

Conversation was slow to start, but once Brady began telling stories about his early days working with Winnie, the girls became more animated. Even Brook, who was a much tougher audience than her younger sister. By the end of the meal, the noodles had been consumed, most of the green beans had somehow disappeared, though she suspected a good portion were slipped under the table to Winnie, who lay waiting patiently at Brady's feet, and the mood was relaxed. Cassie felt truly at ease for the first time since they walked into the party at the Daniels Canine Academy.

Brady had coaxed the girls into helping him clear the dishes when she heard her phone chime. Glancing around, she spotted it on the countertop faceup in the midst of the upheaval she'd created in putting this meal together. Brady's head turned too, and she knew he'd scanned the notification because his entire body stiffened. He set the plates down on the counter with a clatter, and she rose from her chair.

"What? What is it?" she demanded, stretching her arm out in a gesture for him to hand over the phone.

It chimed three more times in rapid succession.

Brady waved her into her seat and checked the notifications again. Then he looked at Cassie with troubled eyes as he pressed the button to lock the screen again. But he didn't hand it over. She sank down into her chair, and he pivoted to the girls, who were jostling for position at the sink.

"Hey, since your mom worked so hard at cooking this great dinner, and I'm sure you girls helped," he added, fixing them with a pointed stare.

They hadn't helped at all. Cassie had to stifle a grin as she watched them wrestle with telling the truth or letting him go on believing they'd been angels.

Thankfully, he plowed ahead, oblivious to their consternation. "How about I put you to work too? Go put on long pants and your sturdiest tennis shoes, okay?"

Brook frowned and glanced at the window dubiously. "Long pants? It's summer."

Brady grimaced an acknowledgment to the season. "I know, but we always wear long pants and sturdy shoes when we're near a construction site," he informed them gravely. "It's important for the safety of the crew. If you want to be on my crew, then you've got to wear the uniform." He looked at Cassie, then pointed at the window with the view of the home under construction. "I wanna show you what my house will look like."

The girls took off for the room they were sharing, jabbering all the way about who was gonna be the boss of who on Brady's crew.

They both winced when the bedroom door slammed shut. Brady grabbed the phone and handed it to Cassie. She wanted to compliment him on how good he was with her daughters, but her curiosity couldn't be contained. Unlocking the phone, she opened her messaging app to see the stream of texts that had obviously upset Brady.

Don't you think you should come home?

I'm tired of chasing you around.

This town isn't that big.

Do you think I can't find you?

Cassie tried to suppress the shudder of terror that raced down her spine. At a loss for what to say, she asked the question she'd had looping through her head for days. "What is it about me?" She spoke barely above a whisper, her gaze fixed on the phone. "How do I always get mixed up with these guys? I think I'm a good person. I work hard, I'm doing my best to raise my girls the best way I can…to make them good people—"

She choked on the last word. Tears filled her vision, but she pressed the heels of her hands to her eyes to stop them. She didn't want to cry. She was angry, not sad or scared. She was stronger than tears. She wanted to find Keith Norton and drag him off into the woods. Leave him there scared and unprotected. Terrify him the way he'd terrified her children.

A blur of black moved into her field of vision. She lowered her hands, frustration bubbling inside her when she felt two hot drops spill over her lashes and course their way down her cheeks. Keith had made her see red, but now all she saw was Brady kneeling in front of her, strong and steady, his expression sincere.

"It isn't you, Cassie. It's them. None of this is your fault. There are as many good people out there as there are bad people." He stopped, tensing his jaw against his own emotions.

What were they exactly? she wondered. Did he feel the same anger and frustration roiling inside her? He must have.

He drew a deep breath and exhaled slowly before pressing on. "Unfortunately, you've run into a couple of pretty bad ones. But it isn't you. You haven't done anything wrong."

A sob rose up and strangled her. She placed her hand over her mouth to catch the damn thing. She wasn't going to cry. Forcing herself to take deep breaths in through her nose and out through her mouth, she held Brady's gaze until she felt she could speak.

When she did, her voice cracked, but she held the tears in check. "How can you be sure? What if I'm some kind of a magnet for trouble?" she asked, allowing this calm, steady man to hear her deepest fear.

She trusted Brady when she had no reason to trust any man. And she'd upended his entire life with her drama.

Brady dropped back and landed on his rump. Winnie commando-crawled out from under the table. She gave his cheek a sniff, then turned to face Cassie. The dog sat patiently staring at her, clearly intending to take over where her partner wasn't getting the job done.

She put out a tentative paw, and Cassie broke.

Laughing and crying all at once, she hugged the dog

the way she wished she could hug Brady. "Oh, sweet girl. I don't want to get your fur all wet again."

Brady looked at her from his spot on the floor. "Labradors are water dogs. They don't mind getting wet."

Bracing the dog's soft cheeks between her palms, Cassie stared into Winnie soulful eyes. "Thank you. You're such a good girl. I won't even tell the boss man there about the green beans you've been eating all night."

Brady chuckled. "There are worse things they could have been giving her," he said with a shrug. "But we're gonna have to talk about table scraps."

The dog turned and shot him a baleful look. Sometimes he thought she understood every word he'd said. Brady gave her midsection a brisk rub. "Labs tend to put on weight, so I have to watch her diet pretty carefully. She needs to be agile when moving through tight spaces."

Cassie wiped the remnants of her tears from her eyes. Straightening her shoulders, she gave him a brisk nod. "I'll explain to the girls. Hopefully, we'll be out of your hair soon and you won't have to worry about having such bad influences around." She forced herself to stand. "You're a good girl," she said, giving Winnie's head one last pat.

Brady's expression sobered as he scrambled to his feet. "You're staying here until Norton has been caught," he stated in a no-nonsense tone.

Cassie didn't see the point in fighting him when she had absolutely no intention of leaving until his stated outcome had been achieved. "Of course, we are. I can't think of any place the girls and I would feel safer than right here with you and Winnie."

Her cheeks heated with the admission, but she refused to look away. It was the truth, and the trials and tribulations of her past had taught her that pride was a cheap commodity.

And truth was worth its weight in gold.

Brady held out a hand for her to shake, prepared to seal their pact. Cassie took it, loving the way the warmth of his fingers enveloped hers. She was not a tiny or incapable woman, but there was something about Brady's presence. He made her feel protected but not diminished.

Shaking her head to dislodge those thoughts, she glanced at her phone. "Should I block the number?"

Brady gave his uniform pants a cursory brush, then shook his head. "No. I think it's best to let him see the text came through and was read. The last thing we want is for him to disappear for a while. We want him to stay right here until we can catch him. Otherwise, you'll be waiting and watching, wondering if he plans to return." Brady reached out and gave her shoulder a squeeze. "This is scary, but you came here to build a new life. I want you to be able to get on with your life without needing to look over your shoulder constantly."

Cassie pushed the phone to the corner of the counter. "Okay. I'll leave it open, but I'm not going to respond."

"He will see the read receipt. It'll be good enough. He's getting anxious to find you. I spoke to the chief this afternoon, and I'm going to be taking a couple of days off to stick close to home."

Cassie shook her head, her ponytail flying. "Oh, Brady, you don't have to take vacation days. We can take care of ourselves."

"You absolutely can, but until this is over, Chief Walters and I think it would be best if either Winnie or I are on-site." He looked her straight in the eye. "He's going to make a move soon. I feel it in my bones."

"You don't think he'll find us out here, do you?"

He pinned her with a stare. "I think he's going to go anywhere you are. I am too." He paused, wondering if she was playing his words over in her mind. "But I don't mean in a creepy way," he added quickly.

She grinned when she saw him tug at one pink ear. "Right. No, I get you. And thank you. Your noncreepy presence makes us all feel a lot better."

Chapter Twenty-Four

Cassie dressed in a pair of dark skinny jeans and hiking boots for the excursion to the backyard. The girls had also complied with Brady's uniform regulations, though she doubted any of his regular helpers rocked rhinestone unicorns on the legs of their jeans or silky flowers appliquéd to their rear pockets.

When they stepped out onto the deck, they found him waiting at the foot of the stairs wearing a faded gray T-shirt and jeans he'd obviously worn to paint at some point. Cassie did her best not to ogle the man as he plunked two bright yellow hard hats onto the girls' heads.

They were too big, of course, which sent them into gales of giggles. Brady grinned as he took the hats and adjusted them to their smallest fit. Once he was satisfied, he scooped two more hard hats up off the ground. He placed a white one covered in scuff marks on his own head, then handed her a dull blue hat that appeared to have seen many years of service.

"Sorry, I had to scrounge through what I had around."

Cassie tried the hat on for size. It fit decently enough, though she was sure she didn't look anywhere near as cute as the girls did in theirs. "Nothing we can't cure with glitter glue and some stickers, right, girls?" she asked, shooting him a mischievous glance.

The girls cheered their approval for the plan, but Brady shook his head. "I'm afraid I can't allow glitter glue and stickers. You're wearing Dillon's hat, and he is definitely more into airbrush painting." He gestured for them to join him in the yard with a wave of his arm.

"Come on down." As they started down the steps, he spoke reassuringly. "I put away most of the tools and any miscellaneous hardware I could find laying around the place, but it's really important you girls never play out here without either me or your mom with you. There are dangerous tools out here. I would be upset if you were hurt, and Winnie would probably never forgive me." He jerked his head toward the dog, who had settled herself in a sunny patch of grass a few feet away. "Do we have a deal?"

Both girls nodded, their bright yellow hard hats slipping down over their eyes and making them giggle again. Jilly's tumbled to the ground, but she scooped it from the dirt and slapped it onto her skull with such force Cassie winced.

Brady laughed. "Easy, now. I don't need you hurting yourself with the safety equipment either."

With another wave of his arm, he herded them in the direction of the house under construction. "As I said, I planned a pretty big layout. Mainly because I didn't want to have to add on to it later if I want more room." He glanced down at Brook and flashed her a conspiratorial grin as he tapped the top of her hard hat. "Go big or go home, right?"

"Right," Jilly cried enthusiastically.

As they moved to stand in front of the partially framed structure, he gestured to an opening at the center. "This will be the front door. I plan on building a wraparound porch. At least three sides, if not the whole house. I'm still debating about what to do in the rear of the house. I'd hate to have to clear too many more trees. They're one of the reasons I bought the place." He pointed to his left. "There's a trail down to Cade's Creek."

"Nice," Cassie murmured.

"I might go with more of a side yard," he continued, gesturing to the open area to their right. "I'm thinking of putting in a pond or a pool."

"Oh!" Jilly gasped.

Brook bounced with excitement beside her. "A pool! A pool!" she exclaimed, clapping her hands together.

Brady stroked his chin, then smoothed his neatly clipped beard down his throat. "You think?" he asked, cocking his head to the side, surveying the area and weighing the possibilities. "I was thinking a small pond would be cool. I could stock it with some fish, maybe build a dock to sit on in case I want to toss a line in."

The hopeful note in his tone made Cassie's heart pound. She could envision him sitting on his imaginary dock. "Sounds nice. And you can also swim in a pond," she added for the girls' benefit.

Brook stilled, staring at Brady solemnly. "A pool would be prettier."

Brady pursed his lips, like he was seriously taking her point under consideration. "Yes, a pool would be prettier. But Winnie loves a pond. She likes to swim."

Jilly's whole demeanor changed at the mention of the dog's name. "Oh yeah. Winnie would like a pond better," she agreed like she was an authority on his dog's swimming preferences.

Brady steered the conversation to the house again. "Okay, follow me." They fell into a line like ducklings, with Cassie bringing up the rear. She wanted to be sure the girls didn't stray too far off whatever path Brady determined was suitable.

He led them through the maze of walls, pointing out which rooms would be where, but she was hard-pressed to visualize the final layout. His enthusiasm was distracting. *He* was distracting. When the brief tour was over, she asked, "Do you have actual plans drawn out?"

"Yeah. I took my ideas into an architectural firm in Boise, and they gave me a set of blueprints."

"But you designed it yourself," she said, impressed.

"For the most part." He shrugged. "One of the architects made a couple of suggestions, which made sense. I was open to input."

"Amazing."

Cassie didn't mean it was amazing he designed the house himself, but his willingness to be open to input from others. Another way that Brady Nichols stood apart from other men. When they returned to the double-wide, Brady collected their hard hats in a stack and set them on the deck. In the waning evening light, Cassie could see the weariness around his eyes, and she decided Brady might appreciate some space to relax. Clapping her hands to get the girls' attention, she made a shooing motion toward the door. "Okay, dessert then bath time," she announced.

The girls groaned when she mentioned the bath, but Cassie ignored it as usual. "You know the drill." She leaned down to whisper to Jilly, whose bottom lip stood out in a pronounced pout, "You don't want Winnie to think you stink, do you?"

She scooped out bowls of ice cream for all of them. She smiled when Brady seated himself at the table, clearly as excited about dessert as the girls were. She took her own bowl and dropped back into the chair she was starting to think of as hers. A dangerous presumption, she knew. But here, seated at this small table with these three people, she felt safe.

The scraping of spoons against empty bowls brought her out of her haze. Giving the table a firm pat, she announced, "Okay. To the bath, ladies."

Jilly was off like a shot, calling out her demands for bubblegum-scented bubble bath. She'd spotted the bottle Cassie had purchased on their grocery store visit, and seemed to be determined to use it all as fast as possible.

She turned to look at Brook and caught the older girl rolling her eyes in exasperation. "Can I take a shower instead?" she asked in a hushed tone. "I'm getting kind of big for baths."

Cassie's heart clenched. Another rite of passage. Another reminder her eldest was a big girl now, and running headlong into those preteen days where they would start to clash.

"Sure," she said, running her hand over Brook's long ponytail. "Let me get Jilly out of the way, then it's all yours."

Brook followed her sister into the trailer. She swallowed down the lump of emotion, focusing on the spot where the sun set beyond the trees.

"Too fast," she murmured to herself.

But Brady heard her and stepped closer. Truthfully, she'd forgotten about Brady until he placed a comforting hand on her shoulder. "Nah, she's only trying to be different."

Cassie shifted to look at him. She appreciated his attempts to make her feel better, but she had far more experience at turning from a girl into a young woman than the man beside her.

"I'd better go supervise, or Jilly will dump the entire bottle into your tub."

He gave her room to move past him. "Yeah, good idea. I bought this place as is, and I'm not sure how well the plumbing will handle being bubble-gummed," he said, pulling a face.

Loath to miss the sunset lighting the woods, she turned to him. "We'll be out of your hair soon, I promise," she said.

"I grabbed a bottle of wine at the store, if you'd like a glass once the girls are in bed," he said, speaking over her promises.

Their eyes met and held. Brady broke the tension.

"You're not in my hair. I like having you here. I didn't realize how quiet the place was," he said sincerely.

A squeal reverberated through the trailer, and Cassie grimaced. "Certainly not quiet anymore. Thanks for the tour, and a glass of wine would be great."

Chapter Twenty-Five

By the time Cassie got the girls settled, full dark had come to the foothills and Brady Nichols had moved to the porch. Padding silently through the house on bare feet, she double-checked the locks on the kitchen window and the back door to be sure. Then she tugged the hem of her T-shirt down and made a futile attempt to press the wrinkles from her shorts with the steam from her sweaty palms.

Running back to her room to primp would be too obvious, so she unleashed a long sigh and smoothed her hair before stepping out onto the porch. A single citronella candle burned in a bucket at the far end away from the steps. Brady sat on the top step, his long legs stretched out in front of him. He had a bottle of beer on the step between his knees and an old-fashioned jelly jar filled with pink wine beside him. She smiled when she saw he'd taken the trouble to cover the top of the glass with a paper napkin.

He looked up when she set foot on the porch. "I didn't want to turn on any lights. We'd attract every bug from here to Boise."

"Good thinking." She pointed to the jar of wine.

"Fancy stemware," she said, unable to suppress a grin. "If I didn't know any better, I'd think you were trying to impress me."

"Maybe I am." Brady reached over and picked up the wine he'd poured for her. Whipping the napkin off with a flourish, he raised both eyebrows and announced, "Only the best for you, *mah-dahm*."

Cassie snickered and accepted the jar. "Thank you, kind sir," she said, settling down beside him. "The girls have been making you play Princess and the Dragon too much."

"I'm hoping it'll be my turn to be the dragon soon," he said, his expression impressively neutral.

Chuckling, Cassie tipped the jelly jar to her lips. The wine was cool and fruity. The perfect antidote to the sticky warmth of the hectic summer day. A wry smile twisted her lips. "It's funny, I never think to buy myself wine."

"I have beer, if you'd rather have one of those," Brady said, tensing to rise. "And, you know, water and stuff."

She shook her head hard, and he paused as if in suspended animation. "The wine is perfect. Thank you."

They sat together in companionable silence for a few minutes. Cassie gazed out into the velvet darkness, mesmerized by how thick and warm the night felt as it closed in around them. Part of her knew she should be wary. She was out in the middle of nowhere, alone with a man who was practically a stranger. But she wasn't scared.

She stole a glance at Brady out of the corner of her eye. He was staring into the deep, dark distance as well.

"I'd forgotten how close the night feels when you're

away from the lights of town." She hesitated for a moment, then plunged ahead, finishing the thought. "Like it's a tiger crouched *right there*, ready to pounce."

He jerked as if she'd poked him, then shifted away from her ever so slightly. "We can go back in if you'd feel safer."

But she didn't feel unsafe. For the first time in a long time, she felt absolutely secure. And at that moment, all she wanted to do was sit on those narrow porch steps with this handsome man and bask in the comfort of his presence.

"No, it's beautiful."

"I wouldn't blame you for feeling a little twitchy. I'd never lived anywhere but in a city until I moved out here," he told her, his lips curving into a bashful smile. "The first few nights I lived here, I must have jumped out of my skin at least a half dozen times."

Heartened by his confession, she beamed up at the carpet of brilliant stars gracing the summer sky. "Is that why you decided to get Winnie? So you'd have a companion?"

"Maybe partly," he conceded. "The department has close ties to the Daniels Canine Academy, and I was always impressed with what these dogs can do. When they asked if I wanted to train to be a handler, it might have crossed my mind that I wouldn't be out here alone anymore."

"I can't believe a big, strong man like you would be afraid," she teased, affecting a husky parody of a drawl.

But whatever Brady was going to say in response was interrupted by the buzzing of her phone. She looked down at the device, wariness crawling up her spine as she watched it vibrate across the wooden stair, inching its way closer to Brady's beer bottle.

Brady looked down too. "Unknown caller?"

She shrugged. "I get as many of those as anybody does, I guess. Except now, I always wonder if maybe it's Keith rather than someone trying to sucker me into loan consolidation or sell me a car warranty."

Brady nodded solemnly. "Do you ever answer them?"

She shook her head. "No. I figure if it's somebody who really needs to speak to me, they'll leave a message."

Brady nodded. "I get one every once in a while, but they're not too bad for me." He toasted her. "Maybe they sense I'm a cop."

He lifted his beer bottle to his lips and took a long pull. Cassie caught herself staring at his Adam's apple as he swallowed and forced herself to look away before he caught her gawping.

Grasping for a change of subject, she latched on to the one that was always uppermost in her mind. "The girls really love staying here. Winnie's curled up at the foot of their bed, and they're arguing over which one of them she's protecting."

"Both of them," he said without hesitation.

Cassie nodded. "I told them that, but they're not in the mood to share right now, so I'm afraid that Winnie is going to have to pick sides."

Brady chuckled. "I wonder—"

His speculation was cut off by the vibration of her phone again. They watched as the notification flashed on the screen. Cassie stiffened when she noticed the area code: 406.

The call was coming from Montana.

Brady must have felt her tension because he immediately went on high alert. "What? What is it? Do you recognize that number?"

"No," she reassured him quickly. "It's just, that's the area code for Montana."

"Where? What area of Montana?" he demanded, setting the beer bottle down with a thud.

She shrugged. "The whole state."

"The whole state?" he repeated, incredulous. "A state that big only has one area code?" he asked.

Cassie smirked. "Big state, small population."

"But you don't know the phone number," he pressed.

She shook her head. "Like I said, I get some of those autodialers. I bought this phone in Montana, and lots of them have software that clones phone numbers with similar exchanges so you'll think it's someone you know calling."

His shoulders slumped, but at last he nodded a concession. "Maybe we should go in," he suggested, his voice gruff.

They probably should. It seemed foolish and dangerous for them to be sitting out in the open like this. Especially with Keith still out there. Anger surged through her, and impulsively she reached over and placed a hand on his forearm to restrain him. "No. I want to enjoy this glass of wine and this nice night. I want to sit here in the quiet and just…be."

His brow furrowed, but he nodded slowly. "Do you… Should *I* go inside?"

The soft sincerity of his question gave her the courage to look directly at him. "No. I want to sit here and enjoy this nice, quiet summer night with you."

They subsided into silence once again. Cassie sipped her wine, smiling as the crisp liquid tickled her taste buds. It was nice of him to have thought to buy a bottle. Then again, *he* was nice, so it made sense for him to be thoughtful as well. And sitting there with him, all warm and solid beside her, was somewhere beyond the definition of nice.

"Brady, I—"

Whatever she was going to say was disrupted by a chime indicating that her last caller had indeed left a voice mail.

Growling with frustration, she set her jelly jar down and snatched the phone from the step. "Seriously, if this is someone trying to sell me vinyl siding, I'm probably going to lose my ever-lovin' "

"How dare you sic the cops on me," a deep voice erupted from the speaker. "Who do you think you are? You told them I stole my own kids? I can't steal my own kids—they're my kids," Mark Whitaker said, slurring heavily. "I can see my kids whenever the hell I feel like seeing my kids. If I wanted them, I could just come take them, and you couldn't say anything about it, Miss High and Mighty. You can't sic the cops on me. I'm their father. I have rights. You think twice before you go pointing the police in my direction. My own damn kids," he mumbled before the recording came to a stop.

Cassie stared at the phone, her cheeks aflame and the blood pulsing loud in her ears. She closed her eyes and wished as hard as she could for the porch to cave in and swallow her up.

"Oh, my God," she whispered.

"I take it that was your ex," Brady said as he thrust to his feet.

Cassie's head jerked up and she watched as he stepped down onto the gravel drive and began to pace back and forth in front of the stairs.

"Uh, well, yeah. That was the prize known as Mark Whitaker. Can I pick 'em or can I pick 'em?"

"First of all, he cannot come and take his children anytime he feels like it," Brady insisted, holding up one finger as if there would be multiple points to his argument.

"He's not going to come and get his children," she assured him. "He hasn't attempted to see them since the day I left. He's just mad because I gave somebody an excuse to question him."

"Second, if he thinks he wants to get anywhere near you or those kids, he's going to have to get through me," Brady said as if she hadn't spoken.

Now, maybe on any another night, Cassie would have appreciated the sentiment, but on this night she was fresh out of patience for male posturing.

"No, he would have to get through *me*," she corrected. He opened his mouth, and she held out her palm to stop him. "I am their mother. I will take care of my children. And while we appreciate everything you have done, and continue to do for us, we're not in the market for a white knight."

Her last assertion seemed to draw him up short. Brady stopped pacing and pivoted to face her squarely. "I'm not trying to be some kind of white knight," he argued. "I'm only saying—"

"I know what you're saying, and it's very kind of you, but I will remind you that *I* am the last line of defense between anybody and my children," she stated unequivocally.

Brady blinked, then took a step back. "Right. Of course. I didn't mean to imply anything else."

Clutching her phone, Cassie rose on unsteady legs. "Listen, it's been a long day." She gave a short laugh. "It's been a long week. Month. Year." Bending over, she picked up the jelly jar and held it aloft in salute. "Thank you for the wine, Brady. You're a good man." She raised the jar to her mouth and drained the thing dry in three gulps. Smacking her lips as she lowered it, she flashed him a satisfied smile. "Sometimes you're too good to be real."

"I'm not that good," he retorted.

She knew he wanted to say more, but at that moment, the phone buzzed in her hand. Again, the 406 area code preceded another string of unfamiliar numbers. Turning the screen to face him, she said, "You're far too good to have to deal with me and all the nasty baggage I tote around with me."

Pressing the button on the top of the phone, she held it down until the option to power it off appeared. With a swipe of her thumb, she ended their night. "Good night, Brady. Sleep well. Tomorrow is sure to be another doozy of a day."

With that, she turned on her heel and slipped back into the house. Shoving her blessedly silent phone into her pocket, she headed straight for the hall leading to the bedrooms. When she peeked in the first doorway on the left, she found the girls curled up together like kittens, and their guard dog blinking blearily. Cassie exhaled long and soft when Winnie gave her a reassuring thump of her tail, then settled her chin on her paws again.

"Such good girls," she whispered to the three of them. "Sweet dreams."

Minutes later, she was scrubbed clean and stretched out on the guest bed, wide-awake and listening for things that bumped in the night. The last thing she heard before drifting off to sleep was the creak of Brady's footsteps as he paused outside each of their bedrooms, then quietly closed the door to his.

Chapter Twenty-Six

Brady enjoyed having the Whitaker girls at his place. Or maybe it had been him and Winnie alone out there for too long. Whatever the reason, having them stay under his roof charged him up. They were like firecrackers, adding spark to the day and keeping everyone on their toes.

The day after Mark Whitaker's call, things had been a bit tense with Cassie, so he focused more on the girls. He put Brook and Jilly to work. First, it was stacking small pieces of scrap wood off to the side of the deck. Then, when they grew restless, he took them around to the front of the trailer where a small flower bed planted with evergreens was slowly being overtaken by weeds. For once, he was grateful for the never-ending list of tasks he never got around to tackling. What he considered a trial, they saw as a treat.

Jilly was gleeful at the thought of being allowed to destroy something without getting in trouble. She was born to be a weeder. True to her nature, Brook moved at a slower, more methodical pace. Brady wasn't surprised when he came to check on them and found Brook had refused to pull some of the weeds because they were flowering.

"They're too pretty," she insisted, gazing at him with sincerity lighting her face.

He couldn't disagree with her assessment, so he left the landscaping to her more appreciative eye. When he came around again, he found Cassie settled down in the dirt beside them. He couldn't help remembering how his ex-wife had tossed a houseplant someone had given them as a gift into the trash because she thought it would be "too much trouble."

He commented on Cassie's willingness to get her hands dirty, and she laughed at him outright, her eyes dancing with amusement.

"I'm training to be a river guide and a hiking trail expert. You think I'm afraid of your landscaping?"

Brady could only shake his head as he walked away, grateful the tension from the previous evening had dissipated. She wanted to be a river guide. The notion of her heading off into the wild with a bunch of strangers both terrified and intrigued him. Sure, he'd made a study of her lithe, athletic grace, but it was still hard for him to believe such a beautiful woman derived so much pleasure from the outdoors. His ex-wife, Lisa, had been anything but the outdoorsy type.

Cassie and her girls were a refreshing contrast.

He kept himself busy through the morning by doing parts of the framing he could handle on his own. When the sun had reached its apex, he knew they should find cooler modes of entertainment.

He walked into the kitchen to find Cassie preparing an assembly line of sandwiches. Two of them were peanut butter and jelly, but the other two were piled high with sliced deli meat and cheese. She glanced over her shoulder and waved a butter knife in greeting when she saw him. "I was about to yell out there to ask if you like mayo or mustard on your sandwich," she said.

"Actually, neither," he admitted. Walking over to the fridge, he opened the door and pulled out a bottle of ranch dressing. "I usually squirt some ranch on there. Gives it extra zing."

Cassie looked at the bottle of salad dressing, then down at the jar of mayonnaise on the counter. "Ranch," she said slowly, almost tasting the world. Then she thrust her hand toward him. "Such a guy thing, but not necessarily a bad idea."

Brady handed the bottle over to her, then shoved his hands into the pockets of his jeans. "I'm full of them."

"Listen, Brady, I'm sorry I got a little prickly last night. Living with Mark… Well, let's just say it wasn't the best thing for my self-esteem—"

"No need to apologize," he interrupted.

"No, there is." She turned to look him in the eye. "I have a bit of a chip on my shoulder when it comes to the girls. Or more like, when it comes to me being a good mom."

"You're a great mom," he said quickly.

"I try," she answered with a wan smile. "But I know I get a little sticky about it sometimes." She made a cringing face. "Vera called me out on it, and as much as I hate to admit it, she's right. I tend to take the independence thing a step too far."

She placed her hand on his arm. His gaze flew to hers.

"You have been nothing but good and generous with us, and I want you to know I appreciate you."

He gave a solemn nod. "It's my pleasure. I like having you here."

His statement hung in the air a moment too long. Cassie drew her hand away, curling her fingers into a ball as she turned her attention back to the sandwiches.

Kicking himself for making her uncomfortable, he switched gears entirely.

"Anyway, no worries. We're good, right?"

"Yeah, right. Definitely okay."

"Great." He clapped his hands once, then rubbed his palms together. "So, I was coming in to see if maybe you and your squad would like to go with me to do some fishing down at Cade's Creek. There's lots of shade there, and the trail is an easy walk through the woods."

Cassie's face lit up. "Sounds great."

"There's a nice spot on the bank. If you want, we could make it a picnic."

"Oh, the girls will be so excited," she said, looking up from her work with a grin. "I'll get the food together. You go tell them what the plan is."

Minutes later, Brady realized she tricked him into delivering news that was sure to have taken years off his hearing ability. The girls both squealed and jumped around him like their legs were spring-loaded. He disentangled himself with the excuse of needing to go change into some shorts as they were talking a mile a minute about all the fish they would catch and how they'd ask their mom to cook them for supper.

Pleased with himself, Brady quickly changed and

hurried out to find them assembled near the door. "I guess you're ready."

"We're ready," Brook and Jilly chorused.

Jilly kept a steady run of chatter as he carried the cooler Cassie had packed and led their merry band around the partially constructed house and down the trail leading to the creek.

Once again, Cassie found herself in the rear of their contingent, a couple of fishing rods and a tackle box in hand. Winnie darted ahead of them, scoping the path with her supersnozzle and clearing the way for their safe procession. But Brook grew quieter and more withdrawn as they neared the water.

He claimed to need a minute to rest, and they stepped into a small clearing. Cassie was busy restraining Jilly, who insisted she should run ahead to keep Winnie company, but Brady was focused on Brook. She was almost completely silent, her expression wary and her body language closed. Brady shot a glance at Cassie.

Cassie hushed Jilly with a stern, "No, and that's final."

He stepped away as she abandoned the fishing poles and other equipment in favor of wrapping her arms around Brook's shoulders.

"Are you okay, sweetie?" she asked, keeping her tone light even though her eyes were searching, intense with worry. "Too hot to walk?"

She looked at her mother, her eyes wide and frightened. "I don't like it here."

Cassie hugged her, though her expression said she wasn't entirely clear as to what triggered Brook's apprehension. She appeared to be ready to give those tender emotions a gentle prod when Winnie let out three sharp barks.

Brady straightened. Those weren't happy barks. Those barks meant business.

"Here in the woods? Or at Brady's house?" Cassie probed, her focus locked on her daughter.

Brook shook her head so hard, her entire body twisted with it. "No, I love Brady's house." She looked down at her dusty sandals, then admitted, "I hate the woods."

"All woods or just these woods?" Cassie pressed, but gently.

"All woods," Brook answered in a lisping whisper.

"Okay, then, we don't have to go through them," Cassie asserted, glancing up at Brady.

"You know what?" he said, straining to keep his tone light. "I think I got too hot working on the house and walking down here. I'm getting a headache," he added, holding himself still as Winnie sounded the alert again.

"Aww," Jilly groaned, sensing the outing was about to get nixed.

Cassie tipped her head to look at him, concern written all over her face. "Are you okay? Do you need water?"

Winnie barked again. Three barks. Short, stubborn and insistent, and Brady took a step in the direction of the sound.

Cassie rose to her feet, keeping a hand on Brook's shoulder and reaching out to corral Jilly. "Oh."

"Do you mind if we eat lunch at the house and save the picnic for another day?" Anticipating Jilly's protest, he grabbed the abandoned tackle box and practically shoved it into her skinny arms. "I promise we'll go another day."

Winnie barked again, and both girls turned toward the sound.

Not wanting to freak Brook out any more than she already was, he forced a neutral expression. "She gets excited about the water too." He scooped the poles from the ground and thrust them at Brook, figuring she'd do better with a task. "You girls head to the house. I'll go get her and grab the cooler on the way home."

Cassie placed a hand on each girl and propelled them toward the house, impervious to Jilly's complaints. Brady leaned in at the last second and handed her his house key. "Lock the doors after you."

She gave a barely perceptible nod and nudged the girls ahead. He waited until they were around a bend, then quick-timed it down the rough trail to the stream.

He burst from the tree line as Winnie let loose another barrage of barks.

"I'm here. I'm here," he wheezed, skidding to a halt. He scanned the area but couldn't spot anything amiss. "What is it? What do you have?"

Winnie circled a spot not far from him, then walked toward the trail.

"You got something? Has someone been here?"

He forced himself to take calming breaths and focus on the scene around him. There was no trash or sign of any disturbance of the earth. No one had pitched a tent or built a fire. Winnie pawed the ground, then looked at him expectantly. Unfortunately, his sense of smell was not nearly as keen as hers. But she was trained to discern one human scent from another, and the last person she'd searched for had been Keith Norton, when they checked the lumberyard.

He swore under his breath as he took another look around. "I've got nothing to go on here, girl," he said, holding his hands out in a helpless shrug. "Go. Show me where he went."

Not needing to be asked twice, Winnie turned and bounded toward the trail leading to his property. To the place where he'd sent Cassie and the girls.

A gushing stream of self-recrimination ran through his head as he and Winnie sprinted through the underbrush. They had almost made it to the clearing when Winnie veered to the right. But he couldn't follow her lead. Not until he knew they were safe inside. Brady sprinted directly to the door. Cassie must have been watching from the kitchen window because he heard the locks click. The door opened as he hit the top step.

"What did she find? Was it Keith?"

Brady panted, but shook his head. "I'm not sure. Nothing there, but maybe." He glanced over his shoulder and saw Winnie snuffling around in the woods between the trail and the country road. He whistled, and she lifted her head. Two sharp bursts had her sprinting to the house.

Cassie turned away and without another word she opened the freezer, extracted a handful of ice cubes, and dropped them into Winnie's water.

"Where are the girls?" he asked, twisting the bolt into place.

"Brook is lying down. I asked Jilly to keep an eye on her." Her lips twisted. "She's pretty pleased to be her sister's keeper for once."

"I forgot to grab the cooler," he said, still trying to catch his breath.

"Forget it." Pivoting to the fridge, Cassie extracted the meat, cheese and ranch dressing. "Sit. We'll have our picnic right here."

Chapter Twenty-Seven

Sensing trouble, Winnie stuck close to the girls for the rest in the day. When they sat down to eat their reconstructed sandwiches, the Lab sat right beside Brook. Again, Cassie marveled at the empathy the dog seemed to have. She wondered if this was something Emma Daniels had worked with Winnie on, or if it was a God-given gift.

Either way, she was thankful Winnie had such a sharp sense for reading the emotions of those around her. Brady said not all dogs did. But his Winnie was as much about the rescue as she was the search, and Cassie was grateful as she watched Brook wind her thin arms around the dog and bury her face in Winnie's neck.

"I think it should be my turn to hug Winnie now. I haven't hugged her since this morning and she's probably missing me too," Jilly interrupted, oblivious to her older sister's distress.

"I'm sure she is," Cassie said, gently placing a hand on Jilly's head to still the girl.

Brady gathered the plates she'd used for their sandwiches. "I think this picnic was a better idea. I don't really like sitting on the ground anyway," he said a shade too cheerfully. "Ants. Every picnic's uninvited guests."

Cassie almost snickered at the idea of a man like Brady being bothered by a few pesky ants, but she caught herself.

"I don't like ants in my pants either," she said gravely. "Makes me have to do a dance."

"You can't dance." Jilly's laughter bubbled out of her, and soon Brook and Cassie were chuckling along with her.

Cassie might have been insulted by the accusation in her daughter's tone if she weren't so relieved to hear them laugh. "Of course, I can dance," she insisted, highly offended. "Everyone can dance. I bet even Brady can."

"I'm a great dancer."

To prove his skill, he boot-scooted to the sink, then proceeded to do a sort of shuffling cha-cha-slide as he squirted dish soap into the running water. Then and there, Cassie knew she was feeling something more than gratitude to the man who'd literally saved her family.

But she wouldn't dwell on that now. Despite Brook's minimeltdown and Brady's worries about Keith finding out where they were staying, it turned out to be a good day. Or as good as any day was going to be given their circumstances.

Brady had kept the conversation verging on downright silly through the relocated picnic, and Cassie couldn't have been more grateful for the distraction he provided. After lunch, she'd called the therapist recommended by the hospital, spoke to her about Brook's fear of going into the woods, and scheduled an appointment to visit with her the following week.

In the meantime, the woman gave Cassie a few different strategies for getting Brook to talk about what happened when she and Jilly got out of the cave where Keith had left them. She also had some advice on how to help her daughter cope with her emotions when they became too overwhelming. Cassie took copious notes on the last one, planning to put some of those tips to use for herself.

She'd thrown together a homemade pizza for their supper. She'd added a bag salad, and a batch of slice-and-bake cookies to use as the carrot to get her kids to eat the salad. It wasn't the most balanced meal she'd ever prepared, but she felt like they could all use something simple and tasty.

Cassie watched the girls follow Brady and Winnie around the yard like ducklings. He was so good with them. So patient. But she couldn't let her daydreams get too far ahead of her reality. They were temporary guests here. Their abandoned picnic served as a stark reminder of the threat looming over them. Over her.

With a weary sigh, she turned away from the window. She was about to call the girls in for their bath when a text came through on her phone.

It's rude not to answer phone calls, but that's okay. I'll see you soon.

"Keith." She drew in a sharp breath then let it out slowly. Her ex-husband might be annoyed with her, but certainly wasn't going to rouse himself enough to come looking for them. The message had to be from Keith. "Not if I see you first, creep," she muttered.

The door opened, and Brady herded his helpers inside. Oblivious to their chatter, she pointed to the phone on the counter and pointed the protesting girls down the hall. "My code is six-two-three-one," she called over her shoulder. He shot her a puzzled glance, but she simply pointed to the phone again and said, "Six-two-three-one."

She ushered the girls into the hall bath, only half listening to complaints over having to bathe again so soon. Running on autopilot, she used the dirt embedded under their fingernails as proof enough for the need. In truth, she just wanted them close to her.

She was stripping a yammering Jilly from her clothes when Brady's voice reverberated through the door.

"Don't worry yourself over it. It's a mind game."

"I hate games," she shouted over the roar of the water filling the tub.

"I love games," Jilly chirped. "Can we play Uno? I'm so good at Uno," she bragged as she settled into the tub. "Get in with me, Brookie."

All too aware Brook considered herself too big to share a bath with her baby sister these days, Cassie was glad her elder daughter stripped down without a fuss. They were getting too big too fast, and needing her less and less every day. She wanted to be the one they turned to for everything, always. She knew all too soon, they'd edge her out as a member of their magical threesome. Truth be told, she didn't mind the girls' clinginess these past few days.

Cassie handed her elder daughter the bottle of body wash once she was settled in the tub, then she addressed Jilly's question. "I'm not sure if Brady has Uno," she answered, careful to keep it noncommittal.

She sat with her back against the vanity, half listening as the girls debated the merits of various games while steam filled the small bathroom. She shook herself from her stupor and leaned over to turn off the taps. The last thing she wanted was for Brady to discover he had no hot water if he wanted a shower.

"Okay, go ahead. Just a quick dip," she said briskly. "We'll wash hair tomorrow."

The girls cheered at being spared the threat of shampoo in their eyes. As usual, Brook was all business. She finished rinsing the soap from her arms and she stood, letting the water cascade off her and leaving her sister to linger.

She handed her daughter a surprisingly fluffy towel. She caught a whiff and instantly recognized the scent of fabric softener.

"Brady says he's gonna let us hammer," Brook announced as she wound the towel around her body and sat down on the bath mat next to her mother.

"Did he?" Cassie said distractedly. Leaning in, she pecked a quick kiss to her big girl's head and inhaled sharply.

"Yep," Jilly confirmed. "With real hammers and nails."

She was about to quiz them on how this promise had been extracted when she heard a commotion coming from the other end of the house. Winnie began to bark incessantly, and Brady shouted a stream of expletives decidedly unsuitable for impressionable young ears. Both girls turned to look at her, their expressions wide-eyed with wonder and shock.

"Uh-oh," Jilly said under her breath.

"Cassie! Cassie!" Brady called from outside the bathroom door.

Scrambling to her feet, she pressed her cheek to the door. "Yeah? What is it? What's wrong?" she called through the thin barrier of the hollow-core door.

"The house is on fire!" he shouted to her.

"What?" She waved frantically for Jilly to get out of the bath. Brook jumped to her feet and wrapped her own damp towel around her sister, practically hauling the younger girl over the edge of the tub.

"Don't go outside," Brady ordered.

Cassie scowled at the door, her hand flying to her mouth. "What? But we're on fire," she shouted. Swiveling her head to fix the girls with a stern stare meant to hold them in place, she opened the door a crack and called over Winnie's frantic barking, "Brady? Shouldn't we evacuate?"

"Not this house. The new house," he clarified, breathless. "Here," he said, shoving her phone into her hand. "Lock yourselves in."

Winnie continued to bark, racing back and forth in the narrow hall. The white walls glowed a terrifying shade of orange.

Her breath caught in her throat as she pressed the three digits, then held the phone to her ear. She slipped out into the hall and craned her neck to sneak a peek out the kitchen window. A towering flame danced from one of the high support beams and licked at one of the outstretched limbs of a nearby tree.

The dog continued to bark, the sound growing rough and hoarse with each volley. Above it all, the keening wails of her daughters reached out to her. Pressing the phone to her ear harder, she plugged the other ear with her index finger.

At last, Jenny, the county dispatcher, came on the line. "Jasper emergency services. Police, fire or medical emergency?" she said briskly.

"Fire," Cassie blurted. "Fire! Brady Nichols's new house is on fire."

"Brady's house?" Jenny said, the shock in her tone evident.

"Not his current house. The house he's building is on fire," Cassie clarified.

Unable to wrap her mind around what she was saying, she rushed to the kitchen window to look again. She needed to be sure she hadn't imagined the sight of his dream home in flames while she cowered in his double-wide.

She hadn't.

She saw Brady struggling to pull a garden hose free from its coil. The fire looked too far gone for a hose to do much good, and her heart broke for him. "Brady's trying to spray the flames with a hose, but we need help."

"Help is on the way." Jenny paused. "Can you stay on the line with me until they've arrived?"

Cassie backed away from the window. "Yes, but I have to go into the other room. I was giving my daughters a bath," she explained.

"Keep the call connected in case I need to ask any questions," Jenny said, her voice comfortingly calm.

Cassie sneaked one last glance at the window and saw the most pathetic stream of water ever to shoot from a hose dribble out then shrink to a drip on the dry ground at Brady's feet. She realized in an instant the hose must have a hole in it.

"It looks like there's a hole in his hose or something," Cassie reported briskly. "Tell the fire department to hurry —"

She turned to leave the kitchen, but the words died in her throat when she stepped into the hall and saw Keith Norton standing square in the front doorway. As subtly as she could, Cassie lowered the phone from her ear. "Keith, what are you doing here?"

It was a stupid question, she knew, but she needed to stall. She needed to get to safety. More than anything, she needed to get between this man and her girls.

Chapter Twenty-Eight

Brady swore another blue streak as he looked down at the shredded garden hose in his hand. It had been a warm summer, but not hot enough to put so many cracks in a brand-new hose. Winnie's barking became more frantic. He turned away from the dancing flames consuming his hard work to look at the secondhand trailer meant to be a refuge for Cassie and her family.

The family he'd left unattended.

His stomach dropped and his fingers opened. The shredded hose fell to the ground, tangling around his feet.

He'd left them alone, and his hose hadn't cracked from baking in the sun. As he circled the house, the sweeping beam of his flashlight caught on something metal in the woods. Whirling, he swung the beam around until it shone on a red pickup truck parked on the other side of the clearing.

"Son of a—" He took off for the front door in a sprint.

"Cassie!" he called as he bolted into the double-wide. Winnie's ferocious barks nearly drowned out the sound of terrified wails. Almost, but not quite. Reaching into the coat closet, he yanked his utility belt off the high shelf where he'd stored it since two small children invaded his life and his home. He freed both his Taser and his service revolver from their nylon compartments.

Easing into the living room area, he crept forward cautiously. "Cassie! It's a trap," he called to her, though he was sure Norton was already in the house. Winnie stood at the opening of the hallway, her eyes fixed on someone in the narrow passage, and her barking incessant and aggressive. Brady couldn't see him, but it was clear she had Norton cornered.

"I'll shoot the dog," a man shouted from the end of the hall.

Brady closed his eyes, praying Cassie and the girls had managed to barricade themselves in one of the rooms. He didn't believe Norton would shoot Winnie. If the man could kill an animal, he would have done so already. Still, Brady didn't see the point in showing his cards quite yet.

"Don't harm the dog," he called out. "Winnie, down."

On command, the Labrador pressed herself to the floor, but remained poised to pounce. If Norton did have a gun, he wanted Winnie to be as small a target as possible.

Winnie did not stop barking.

Norton spoke again, shouting over the snarls and barks. "I mean it. Make it stop or I'll shoot the damn thing."

Brady moved closer to his partner and spoke in the low, commanding tone she responded to best. "Winnie, quiet."

The Labrador barking came to an abrupt halt, but Winnie wasn't above letting out a high-pitched, keening whine he assumed meant she was not happy with the command. Norton would think he got what he wanted. It was the best Brady could do until he could determine whether the man was truly armed or not.

"I'm a police officer," he called out. "Lieutenant Brady Nichols of the Jasper Police Department, and this is my home." He paused long enough to let the information penetrate. "You are a trespasser in my home. I am armed. If you are armed as well, I suggest you drop your weapon and step out into the open immediately."

"I'm not going anywhere until Cassie is where she belongs," Norton said, an edge of belligerence in his tone.

Brady inched closer to the corner of the hallway. "I'm serious, Norton. We have all your information—where you're from, where you've been. If you are carrying a weapon of any sort, I strongly suggest you drop it now."

"Mama?" one of the girls called in a voice trembling with fear. He wanted to throttle Norton for traumatizing those two sweet, innocent girls in his quest to make a point with a woman who clearly didn't want him.

"Hush, baby," Cassie said from somewhere down the hall. "Hush now, it'll be okay, Brady's here. And Winnie."

Her vote of confidence was all he needed to galvanize him into action. He snapped his fingers once and Winnie sprang into action, barking as loud as he'd ever heard as she ran straight at her target. Brady swung around the corner, his weapon leading the way.

Thankfully, both he and Cassie had closed the bedroom doors. Norton cowered at the end against the wall, too frightened of Winnie to have the guts to try either of the doors. Instead, the man stood pressed against the full-length mirror the previous owner had hung there, his hands raised high above his head.

"Call off your dog. Call off your dog," he said, his demands sharp with panic.

"Winnie, heel." Brady trained his weapon on the man, and smirked when he saw his dog stop with her muzzle within a breath of the man's crotch. She stood with her fur raised along her spine, her eyes fastened on Norton's zipper. He followed Winnie into the narrow passageway. "Cassie? Are you and the girls all right?" he called, not taking his eyes off of Norton.

"We're fine," Cassie yelled. Her words were muffled, and he prayed she was behind a closed and locked door. "But Brady, he has a knife."

No sooner did her words penetrate than Brady saw Norton swing his hand down. He caught the glint of a blade as Norton slashed at his dog, but Winnie was faster than her assailant and her senses more attuned to danger than any human could imagine. The dog shifted onto her haunches, managing to avoid the arc of the knife, but Norton's reflexes weren't nearly as good. The momentum of his swing meant the kitchen knife he held tight in his fist sliced into his own thigh.

Norton crumpled, crying out in pain and dropping the knife as he doubled over to clutch his leg with both hands.

Brady rushed closer, kicking the knife out of Norton's reach with the heel of his work boot. He didn't lower his weapon. "Oh, now you've really made a big mistake," he said, his tone deadly calm and chillingly soft.

Norton looked at him, his expression a mixture of

anger and anguish. "I'm injured," he said, biting off each word.

"Self-inflicted wound," Brady corrected. "You injured yourself in an attempt to assault an officer of the law," he clarified, enunciating each word to be sure they sunk in through the man's thick skull.

"It's a damn dog," Norton ground out between clenched teeth.

"She is Officer Winnie, a duly sworn member of the Jasper Police Department. An assault on her will bring additional charges, though I don't think you'll get off too lightly with the Feds when it comes to the kidnapping attempt."

"I didn't kidnap the girls. They walked away with me. Their mother and I are going to get married," Norton snarled. "They know me. They came with me because we're going to be a family."

Brady shook his head. He wasn't going to argue with a man who was clearly delusional. "You have the right to remain silent," he said as he heard sirens approach in the distance. He finished running through Norton's rights, as footsteps pounded on the porch steps. He was happy to put the safety on his weapon as Jason Wright rushed past him, gripping a set of handcuffs.

"All clear here?" Cal Hoover asked when he and Ruby entered the scene.

Brady's shoulders slumped. "We're all fine," he said brusquely. "Norton injured himself with a knife." He turned to his friend and offered his firearm handle first, his hand trembling as the aftereffects of the adrenaline rush pulsed through him. "Here, can you hold this for me?"

Cal took the gun from Brady. "We're going to step out of here," Cal informed him. "This hallway is tight, and Winnie looks fairly wound up."

Brady glanced at Winnie and saw his dog still hadn't shifted into a position of ease. "Winnie, down, girl. Sit."

At last, the Labrador's rump hit the floor. But she wouldn't take her eyes off Norton while Jason Wright secured the cuffs in front of the injured man.

"JFD is working on your house," Jason informed him. "They pulled in right in front of us." He moved to Norton's injured side and pushed himself under the man's arm. "EMTs are outside. I'll have them take a look at this paper cut, then we'll take him down to the station."

"Cassie," Norton called out as Jason pushed him past the closed bathroom door. "Cassie, let me explain. Give me a chance to ex—"

His words were cut off when the bathroom door flew open and Cassie Whitaker shot out like a bullet fired from Brady's gun.

"Explain? You want to explain kidnapping my daughters and holding them out in the woods overnight in the cold and dark? Are you going to try to tell me you didn't think they would be scared? Or maybe you wanna tell me about how they ran away from you and got lost in the woods, but were still smart enough to find the creek and follow it toward town," she said, raspy with unspent emotion. "There's nothing to explain, Keith. There is nothing between us. We were never serious. I was never going to marry you. Never." She stared him right in the face, a portrait of defiance. "You've stalked me, stolen my children, terrorized us. There's nothing in this world that can make me come within ten feet of you. We will never speak again, Keith. Ever."

Having spoken her piece, she stepped into the bathroom and slammed the door so hard the entire place shook.

Cal let out a low whistle as Jason propelled a sputtering Norton past him. "Man, if a dressing-down like that doesn't make things clear for you, nothing will," he said to the cuffed man.

When he was sure Jason and Norton were out the door, Cal turned to Brady with a nod and said, "How about I take Winnie out for a run in the woods and let her work some of the adrenaline off? We'll head for the road, since the crew is working on putting out the bonfire you've got going on out there." He gave his head a sad shake. "I sure am sorry about the house, Brady."

Brady looked up, numbness setting in as his synapses slowed. "Winnie, go. Go with Cal and Ruby."

The dog followed his order, but not without casting one last, worried glance at Brady. "You're a good girl. The best. Now, go with Cal."

Chapter Twenty-Nine

Once they had gone, Brady stepped forward and knocked on the bathroom door with the knuckle of his index finger. "It's me. Let me in?"

There was a pause, then Cassie asked, "Is everyone else gone?"

Her question was muffled. When he cracked open the door, he found them huddled together. The girls were clad in cotton nightgowns stuck to them where the damp ends of their hair dripped. They were wrapped around their mother like koalas clinging to a tree. "It's me," he assured them.

As always, Jilly was the first to shift gears. Peeling herself away from Cassie, she hurtled into his legs. "Winnie saved us."

Without thinking, Brady reached down to smooth her silky hair, tempted to point out he'd played a small part in holding Keith Norton until backup arrived. But as far as Jilly was concerned, he was merely the guy who scooped kibble for Wonder Winnie, and that was okay with him.

"Winnie is the best."

"So are you," Cassie said, voice hoarse with tears and residual anger.

He glanced over at her. "Thank you." He drew a steadying breath, then said, "We'll book Norton into custody here, but the Bureau will likely take over the case. I'm assuming he'll be moved to Boise for holding."

"Can they send him farther?" Cassie asked with a watery half smile.

"Like to the moon?" Brook grumbled, nuzzling deeper into Cassie.

Jilly immediately latched on to the idea, tipping her small face to his. "Yeah! Like on a rocket."

Brady stared down at her, marveling at the girl's resilience. "Yeah, I think Boise is about as far as we can say for sure, but I'll suggest an interstellar incarceration."

"Sounds too cool for Keith," Cassie grumbled. "He needs to be sent to a place decidedly warmer and fierier—"

She stopped, her eyes widening as she scrambled to her feet, Brook clinging to her. "Oh, my God, Brady, your house!" Standing on her toes, she craned her neck to look out the small window above the tub. But all she could see was the orange glow of fire. "Your beautiful house," she said, fresh worry creasing her brow.

Brady shook his head to indicate there was nothing to be done. Crouching, he swept Jilly into his arms. "I'm not worried about the house."

"But—"

"It's wood and nails, Cassie," he said, the gruff finality in his tone cutting through her arguments. Cradling Jilly's head in the palm of his hand, he found solace in her trusting embrace. "It doesn't matter. All that matters is we're all safe."

Tears filled her big hazel eyes. "Thanks to you."

"Winnie did it," Jilly corrected, her face nuzzled into his neck.

Brady was more than happy to let his partner take the credit. The warmth in Cassie's gaze was more than enough for him. "That's right. Winnie will want you girls to help her make a statement."

He did his best not to turn his head to look at the fire as he led them out of the bathroom and into the smoke-filled twilight. He didn't have to look to know exactly how bad the scene behind the trailer would be. The flames had been subdued, but all around them, fire-fighters continued to shout instructions to one another. A second truck had arrived minutes after the first, but his gut told him their efforts would be too late. Even as Cassie fell into step beside him with Brook clasping her mother's hand tightly, Brady was beginning to accept the reality of his home being beyond saving.

"It's going to be a mess here tonight," he informed Cassie. "Will you be able to stay with Vera and Millard?"

She turned, her gaze following a pair of firefighters in full turnout gear as they sprinted around the corner of the trailer. "I guess we could, but with Keith in custody, I think I'd rather go home. Do you think we can?"

His heart clenched at the hopefulness in her tone. Home. To the house where her grandparents had lived. Home, to the place where she and her daughters would make new memories. If they stayed here.

Lowering Jilly to the ground beside Cal's SUV, he said, "Yeah. Of course. I don't see why not."

"I think the sooner I have the girls in their own beds, the better."

"You're probably right," he agreed, though the words came out gravelly with disappointment. He hated to see them go. All of them. It was bad enough contemplating one night, but now... She was right. There was no reason for them to stay with him. Except he wanted them there.

Mentally kicking himself for letting his own selfish feelings get in the way of what might be best for her poor, traumatized girls, he kept his mouth shut tight as they made their way to the vehicles.

"Do we have to go to the police station again?" Brook asked, trepidation making her voice quaver.

Brady knew they would have to take a statement from Cassie and the girls, but he hadn't thought far enough ahead to request their interview be done as far from where Norton was being held as possible.

Cal stepped out from the other side of the van with Winnie and Ruby straining at their leads and saved him from floundering. "No, miss," he replied, all Western civility. "Unlike some people, you are not under arrest. You are our star witnesses." He met Brady's troubled gaze, and Brady gave a grateful nod. "As such, I think it means you get to choose." Turning to Cassie, he said, "We can conduct our business at your house, if that's okay with you, ma'am."

"Our house would be great. Thank you."

"Can Winnie spend the night with us?" Jilly asked, her face lighting with hope as she turned to Brady.

A sad smile twisted his lips. "I'm sorry. She'd like

it a lot, but she needs to stay with me. We're partners, remember?"

Both girls looked crestfallen. He felt like an ogre, but Winnie was first and foremost a working dog, and as such, constant reinforcement of her routine was essential. "But you are welcome to visit us whenever you like," he said, his gaze drifting to Cassie's and holding. "Anytime. We'll miss having you around."

Cassie returned his stare long enough to make his heart start to hammer. But then she shifted her attention to strapping her daughters into her van. "We will definitely visit, sometime. Maybe even bring Brady some brownies baked in a regular baking pan," she said, injecting a note of forced cheer into her tone.

"I take brownies any way I can get them," he said, matching her false brightness.

When the girls were buckled in, and Cal went to secure Ruby in his vehicle, Brady followed Cassie to the driver's door. "Are you okay to drive?" he asked, glad he didn't need to mask his worry for the sake of the girls.

She gave a laugh, but it sounded more like a sob. "I can't believe you're asking if *I'll* be okay." Shaking her head, she gestured to the chaos surrounding them. "Brady, your house—"

"I told you, the house can be rebuilt." He stepped closer and stared straight into her wide, troubled eyes. "You and the girls are safe. That's all that matters to me."

She wet her lips, and the temptation to kiss her was so strong, he had to make himself move away.

"Thank you," she whispered.

Unable to conjure too many coherent words, he simply jerked his chin in acknowledgment, then reached past her to open the door for her. The sounds of the girls bickering in loud whispers was music to his ears. He'd spent the better part of the last week of his life wrapped in the cocoon of their world, and now he was sad to leave it.

"You go on now. I'll see to this and gather up your stuff and we'll get it over to you." She hesitated, and he gave her a tired smile. "It's okay. I'll see you soon," he promised, though he barely recognized his own voice.

Cassie's lips curved. "See you soon," she promised as she slid behind the wheel.

Brady closed the door, then gave it a final pat. The girls waved as Cassie drove carefully through the vehicles littering his front yard. The lights from the fire engines bounced off the windows of the minivan.

Winnie nuzzled his hand with her damp nose and gave a soft whine, letting him know she was nearby. He stroked her head absently. Cassie's brake lights flashed before she turned onto the road.

He spotted a small hand pressed against the side window in a gesture of farewell. He realized from the positioning of the seats, it had to be Brook and something inside him broke.

Behind him, the home of his dreams was going up in smoke, but somehow, it wasn't as hard as watching the family who'd captured his heart drive away into the night.

Chapter Thirty

It took a couple of days for Cassie to gather everything she wanted to give Brady as a thank-you gift. Secretly, she was hoping he was missing her every bit as much as she and the girls missed him.

Cassie was glad Cal Hoover had been the one to take their statement. The girls had been through enough, and being interviewed by the man who'd helped carry them to safety after the night they were lost in the woods made it easier for them to get comfortable with him. Almost as comfortable as they'd been with Brady. But not quite.

And it felt weird to be in her grandparents' house without them. The place didn't feel right. It wasn't her place. And even with two lively girls, something was missing.

Someone was missing.

Cassie walked out of Saunders's Hardware with big bags of donated building materials with a small, smug smile on her face. "It's nice they're going to help, Mama," Brook said approvingly.

"We're all going to help," Jilly chimed in. "I can hammer. Brady said he was gonna show me how to hammer when we were helping him pick stuff up the other day. I bet he'll let me."

Cassie chuckled at her daughter's confidence and enthusiasm. "I bet he will," she agreed.

They turned the corner and found Dillon Diaz lounging against the side of a pickup truck loaded down with an unusual assortment of tools and equipment. Cassie looked at him questioningly.

Dillon shrugged as he pushed away from the vehicle. "I've been collecting everything anyone was willing to give us to use. The truck with the lumber should be arriving shortly. We should probably get a move on," he said briskly.

Cassie shepherded her girls to the van parked across the street. They followed Dillon's pickup truck north out of town. When they got to the crossroads that led to the Daniels ranch, Cassie hooked a right instead of a left. Her breath hitched when she caught sight of the line of cars turning into Brady's driveway.

Once she and the girls had pulled in, there were easily twelve vehicles parked at odd angles. She was attempting to calm the girls when the man himself stepped out onto the small front porch. Brady shook his head in bewilderment as his friends and neighbors climbed from their vehicles.

Cassie was glad for the cover the crowd created. She wasn't exactly sure how Brady would feel about seeing her or the girls. After all, it was their fault the house he'd been building with his own hands had been turned into a pile of ash.

Captain Walters had been the one to tell her Keith Norton had indeed been transferred into federal custody and taken to Boise for holding. Hearing he wasn't even going to spend one more night in Jasper was a relief. Brook and Jilly had been perturbed when Special Agent Sims came to the house for yet another official interview, but they were becoming old pros at the question-and-answer game.

A part of her worried her children were becoming all too inured to the extraordinary circumstances surrounding them, but the minute the federal agent was gone, they turned into her little girls again—bickering, playing and seeking her out for comfort and counsel as needed.

The commotion of car doors slamming and shouted greetings jarred her from her thoughts. She switched off the engine. Brook and Jilly were too fast for her to contain them, but she didn't mind so much. Anxious to see Brady again, Cassie threw off her seat belt and bailed from the van. The dog at Brady's side sighted them before he did. Winnie gave three happy barks, then launched herself off the porch.

Brady looked perplexed by his dog's sudden defection. He snapped his fingers, called and whistled, but it was to no avail. Winnie had her targets in sight. Cassie witnessed the moment he spotted her daughters. He froze for a second, then he beamed so unreservedly it nearly cracked her heart wide-open.

He waved to them, but she could see his head moving from side to side, scanning the crowd as he came down the steps himself. She hoped he was looking for her.

Some would say it was ridiculous for her to feel so attached to a man after only a few days, but those days had been intense. She knew a woman with her history should be wary. But when their gazes met and held, all her doubts disappeared.

He was happy they came.

So was she.

The previous night she'd told Vera she was comfortable with Brady, but it was more than the ease between them. She trusted him with a surety she felt in her bones. And after a couple days of space, she could admit she wanted him. More, she wanted him to want her. And her girls.

All she needed was the guts to tell him what was in her head and her heart.

But, as was his way, Brady made things easier for her straight off the bat.

"Hey, I missed you," he said, his grin unwavering as he approached. Her lips parted, but no sound came out. The next thing she knew, he was holding her tight against him.

"We missed you too," she whispered, aware her choice of pronoun was a bit of a cop-out, but unable to resist shielding herself if even in the smallest way. She chuckled self-consciously as he loosened his hold enough to look at her. "Though I bet it was a lot quieter."

"Too quiet," he said gruffly. "I liked having you here." He gave her arms a squeeze. "All of you."

"Well, here we are, invading your space again," she said with a watery laugh.

"Cal tells me we've handed everything over to the FBI in terms of the kidnapping. Norton will also have charges of malicious vandalism, breaking and entering and terroristic threatening to contend with, but the investigation is closed and he's the lawyers' problem now."

Cassie shot a look at the double-wide Keith had managed to infiltrate and shuddered. "Brady, I'm so sorry I brought all this to your door. Literally." She gave a short laugh and half-heartedly tried to pull away, but he held firm.

"Don't. Don't apologize for something you didn't do. I'm sorry I wasn't thinking more clearly. He should never have gotten through my door."

"Your house—" she started.

But he cut her off with a quick, hard kiss. Whistles and catcalls erupted around them, and they parted on her soft gasp. Brady pressed his lips together and scowled, but it wasn't enough to make them stop.

But he didn't let her go. His arms wound around her and he pulled her into his warm embrace. "I should apologize, but I don't want to," he whispered into her ear.

"I don't want you to," she said on a rush of breath.

He retreated enough to look her in the eye. "It's too much, too fast, and we were thrown together by circumstance," he said huskily. "I get all this logically, but right now, the logical part of my brain is on hiatus. I've been wanting to kiss you for so long."

"I, uh, me too. You," she stammered.

At a sharp bark, she whipped her head around and saw her daughters staring at them. Jilly, for once in her young life, appeared speechless. Brook, looking horrified by their behavior, cried, "Ew!"

But, despite her protestations, her elder daughter's eyes looked bright and, for the first time in too long, hopeful.

"Oh, Winnie!" Jilly cried, then threw her arms around

the panting dog's neck in an exuberant hug. "They love each other!"

Brady's dog showed her approval with a wide doggy grin. She thumped her tail so hard puffs of dust rose.

Cassie's face heated, but she forced herself to look at Brady. "The critics seem divided," she managed to joke.

He shook his head. "Nah, one of them is trying to play it cool, and the other two couldn't act nonchalant if they tried." He left one arm slung over her shoulder as he surveyed the chaos she'd once again rained down on him. "What's all this?"

"Oh!" Pressing her hand to her flaming cheek, she turned to look at the sea of beaming faces watching them with avid interest. "I, um, everyone wanted to help."

"Help?"

"Dillon told me he and some of the other guys were out here clearing debris and checking the foundation. He said things looked solid, so like I said, people wanted to help. Vera and I talked to some of the folks who came into the diner, and Millard has a friend who works with a construction company out of White Feather. They had some lumber left over from a project they had finished. They're dropping it off here—" she paused as the roar of an engine and the hiss of air brakes filled the air "—now, I guess," she concluded with a laugh.

Brady blinked in apparent disbelief as all around them people started strapping on tool belts and wrestling ladders, table saws and other equipment from truck beds. Cassie turned to check on the girls. She bit her lip as she took in the mayhem, then met his warm brown gaze. "I have to tell you something," she said in a whisper meant only for his ears.

Brady's arm tightened, holding her close to his side. "Yeah?"

The hopeful lilt in the single word buoyed her. Stretching onto her toes, she whispered in his ear, "My middle name is Pandora."

His brows shot high, and an incredulous tilt to his lips. "You're kidding."

She shook her head. "Now you're in on my deepest secret," she told him gravely. "I can be a whole passel of trouble, Brady Nichols."

"Cassandra Pan—"

"Would you look at the teeth on that table saw," she cried out, cutting him off.

Brady chuckled, then kissed her temple. "It's safe with me," he assured her.

"I trust you."

Brady gave her another squeeze. "I can't believe you did all this," he said, his eyes wide with wonder.

Behind them, someone let loose with an indelicate snort. "She isn't Wonder Woman," Vera groused as she trundled past holding what appeared to be a tray of sandwiches. "Plenty of folks helped."

Millard followed in his wife's footsteps, a giant stainless-steel urn in his hands. "Hey, Brady," he said in his usual easy manner. "This here's coffee, but I have a couple cases of bottled water too. The folks at the Stop & Shop are sending over some of those sports drinks as well."

Cassie beamed at Brady's bewildered expression. "Vera's right. Everyone wanted to help."

"But you organized it. I see your fingerprints all over this operation."

He gathered her into his arms and bent his head toward hers, but she braced her hands on his chest to hold him off for one more minute. "It wasn't all me. Dillon did a lot of it."

Brady glanced over to where his best friend was directing groups of volunteers like a seasoned construction foreman. "I appreciate the effort, but I'm not kissing him."

"Emma Daniels helped a lot too."

As if conjured, Emma appeared with the teenage boys who worked for her over the summer. "I just wanted a break from cleaning out kennels," she announced, giving Brady a playful nudge as they walked past. "And don't you dare try to kiss me. I'll sic Winnie on you." The trainer turned and walked backward a few steps, her eyes alight with amusement. "You know she still thinks I'm her alpha."

Brady laughed, but tightened his hold on Cassie.

"But you want to kiss me," Cassie murmured when their gazes met again. She needed to confirm the first kiss hadn't been an impulse on his part.

"Absolutely, I do."

"Ew," Brook said loudly. "He's gonna kiss her again."

"I want him to kiss her," Jilly announced loudly. "I want him to kiss her so we can live here in his new house so Winnie can sleep with me every night."

Cassie squeezed her eyes shut, mortified, but the touch of Brady's lips against hers had them popping open wide again.

He flashed a wide, rakish grin. "I think that sounds like a great plan, Jilly," he answered, still holding Cassie's gaze.

"You can't mean—" she began to protest.

"I can, and I do." Without giving her a minute to recover, he released her and turned to scoop a giggling Jilly into his arms. With the smaller girl settled on his hip, he ran a hand over Brook's hair. Despite her protestations about public displays of affection, she moved into his side without hesitation. He met Cassie's gaze steadily. "It'll take a while to get the house built, but we can use the time for us all to get better acquainted. I think it's a great plan."

When Brook stretched her arm out toward her, Cassie stepped into the four-way embrace. "So, this is how it's going to be, huh?" she asked, tears blurring the edges of her words. "You three ganging up on me?"

"Four," Jilly corrected. "Don't forget Winnie."

Cassie felt something brush her calf and glanced down to see the Labrador sit right between her leg and Brady's, her pink tongue lolling as she gazed adoringly at the tangled knot of them.

"Of course not," Cassie whispered, reaching down to pet the dog's head. "We could never forget Winnie. After all, she's the one who introduced us."

* * * * *

Look for Alpha Tracker, *the next book in*
K-9s *on Patrol,*
coming next month from Cindi Myers!

And if you missed the first two titles, you'll find

Decoy Training *by*
New York Times *bestselling author Caridad Piñeiro*

Sniffing Out Danger
by Elizabeth Heiter

Available now wherever
Harlequin Intrigue books are sold!

WE HOPE YOU ENJOYED
THIS BOOK FROM
HARLEQUIN
INTRIGUE

Seek thrills. Solve crimes. Justice served.

Dive into action-packed stories that will keep you
on the edge of your seat. Solve the crime
and deliver justice at all costs.

6 NEW BOOKS AVAILABLE EVERY MONTH!

#2079 SHERIFF IN THE SADDLE

The Law in Lubbock County • by Delores Fossen

The town wants her to arrest her former boyfriend, bad boy Cullen Brodie, for a murder on his ranch—but Sheriff Leigh Mercer has no evidence and refuses. The search for the killer draws them passionately close again...and into relentless danger. Not only could Leigh lose her job for not collaring Brodie...but they could both lose their lives.

#2080 ALPHA TRACKER

K-9s on Patrol • by Cindi Myers

After lawman Dillon Diaz spent one incredible weekend with the mysterious Roslyn Kern, he's shocked to encounter her months later when he's assigned to rescue an injured hiker in the mountains. Now, battling a fiery blaze and an escaped fugitive, it's up to Dillon and his K-9, Bentley, to protect long-lost Rosie—and Dillon's unborn child.

#2081 EYEWITNESS MAN AND WIFE

A Ree and Quint Novel • by Barb Han

Relentless ATF agent Quint Casey won't let his best lead die with a murdered perp. He and his undercover wife, Agent Ree Sheppard, must secretly home in on a powerful weapons kingpin. But their undeniable attraction is breaking too many rules for them to play this mission safe—or guarantee their survival...

#2082 CLOSING IN ON THE COWBOY

Kings of Coyote Creek • by Carla Cassidy

Rancher Johnny King thought he'd moved on since Chelsea Black broke their engagement and shattered his heart. But with his emotions still raw following his father's murder, Chelsea's return to town and vulnerability touches Johnny's heart. And when a mysterious stalker threatens Chelsea's life, protecting her means risking his heart again for the woman who abandoned him.

#2083 RETRACING THE INVESTIGATION

The Saving Kelby Creek Series • by Tyler Anne Snell

When Sheriff Jones Murphy rescues his daughter and her teacher, the widower is surprised to encounter Cassandra West again—and there's no mistaking she's pregnant. Now someone wants her dead for unleashing a secret that stunned their town. And though his heart is closed, Jones's sense of duty isn't letting anyone hurt what is his.

#2084 CANYON CRIME SCENE

The Lost Girls • by Carol Ericson

Cade Larson needs LAPD fingerprint expert Lori Del Valle's help tracking down his troubled sister. And when fingerprints link Cade's sister to another missing woman—and a potentially nefarious treatment center—Lori volunteers to go undercover. Will their dangerous plan bring a predator to justice or tragically end their reunion?

*Rancher Johnny King thought he'd moved on since
Chelsea Black broke their engagement and shattered
his heart. But with his emotions still raw following
his father's murder, Chelsea's return to town and her
vulnerability touches Johnny's heart. And when a
mysterious stalker threatens Chelsea's life, protecting
her means risking his heart again for the woman
who abandoned him.*

*Read on for a sneak preview of
Closing in on the Cowboy,
the first installment of the
Kings of Coyote Creek miniseries
by* New York Times *bestselling author Carla Cassidy!*

"CHELSEA, WHAT'S GOING ON?" Johnny clutched his cell
phone to his ear and at the same time he sat up and turned
on the lamp on his nightstand.

"That man…that man is here. He tried to b-break in."
The words came amid sobs. "He…he was at my back
d-door and breaking the gl-glass to get in."

"Hang up and call Lane," he instructed as he got out
of bed.

"I…already called, but n-nobody is here yet."

Johnny could hear the abject terror in her voice, and an
icy fear shot through him. "Where are you now?"

"I'm in the kitchen."

"Get to the bathroom and lock yourself in. Do you hear me? Lock yourself in the bathroom, and I'll be there as quickly as I can," he instructed.

"Please hurry. I don't know where he is now, and I'm so scared."

"Just get to the bathroom. Lock the door and don't open it for anyone but me or the police." He hung up and quickly dressed. He then strapped on his gun and left his cabin. Any residual sleepiness he might have felt was instantly gone, replaced by a sharp edge of tension that tightened his chest.

Don't miss
Closing in on the Cowboy *by Carla Cassidy,*
available July 2022 wherever
Harlequin Intrigue books and ebooks are sold.

Harlequin.com

HARLEQUIN

Heartfelt or thrilling, passionate or uplifting—Harlequin is more than just happily-ever-after.

With twelve different series to choose from and new books available every month, you are sure to find stories that will move you, uplift you, inspire and delight you.